MW00982270

Hungers

Other books by Genni Gunn

FICTION
Tracing Iris
On The Road
Thrice Upon a Time

POETRY
Mating in Captivity

TRANSLATION
Devour Me Too
Traveling in the Gait of a Fox

*For Michael,
with thanks +
best wishes*

Hungers

GENNI GUNN

RAINCOAST BOOKS

Vancouver

Copyright © 2002 by Genni Gunn

All rights reserved. No part of this publication may be reproduced or transmitted in any form or by any means, electronic or mechanical, including photocopying, recording or by any information storage and retrieval system now known or to be invented, without permission in writing from the publisher.

Raincoast Books
9050 Shaughnessy Street
Vancouver, British Columbia
Canada, V6P 6E5
www.raincoast.com

In the United States:
Publishers Group West
1700 Fourth Street
Berkeley, California
94710

Raincoast Books gratefully acknowledges the support of the Government of Canada through the Book Publishing Industry Development Program, the Canada Council and the Department of Canadian Heritage. We also acknowledge the assistance of the Province of British Columbia through the British Columbia Arts Council.

Edited by Barbara Kuhne
Text design by Ingrid Paulson
Typeset by Teresa Bubela

National Library of Canada Cataloguing in Publication Data
Gunn, Genni
    Hungers

    ISBN 1-55192-566-4

    I. Title.
PS8563.U572H86 2002   C813'.54   C2002-910546-3
PR9199.3.G792H86 2002

Library of Congress Control Number: 2002091725

At Raincoast Books we are committed to protecting the environment and to the responsible use of natural resources. We are acting on this commitment by working with suppliers and printers to phase out our use of paper produced from ancient forest. This book is one step towards that goal. It is printed on 100% ancient-forest-free paper (100% post-consumer recycled), processed chlorine- and acid-free, and supplied by New Leaf paper. It is printed with vegetable-based inks. For further information, visit our website at www.raincoast.com. We are working with Markets Initiative (www.oldgrowthfree.com) on this project.

1 2 3 4 5 6 7 8 9 10

Printed and bound in Canada by Friesens.

Frank

Contents

Los Desesperados

By the time the plane lands in Puerto Vallarta, both Alice and Morris are drunk. The four Scotches, Alice reasons, were necessary to dispel anxiety. Better than sedatives — you get addicted to those. Morris has gone one further. He averts his eyes, but she can see the beginnings of a conscience in the red rings, the shiny pupils.

"We're here, honey," she says and forces a smile. "I wonder if it's changed much."

"Most likely turned into another American tourist trap." Morris stares, gloomy, out the window, as if reluctant to disembark. Deplane, as the flight attendants say. Always makes Alice think of Jonah and the whale. Open the fangs; spit them out. And before they know it, they're in a taxi, heading for … what … a honeymoon twelve years ago?

"Estancia San Paolo," Morris tells the driver.

"Is new, senor? You know what street?"

Morris hands him an address. The cabbie shrugs and drives. Puerto Vallarta has certainly changed since they were here last. It is now a maze of shops along the cobblestones, advertisements in English. It could be southern California, only the air is more humid, the heat sticky. Everyone's on holiday here, Alice thinks, it's not real. She knows that's not true, of course. There's an industry keeping all these tourists fed and watered and sheltered and amused. Like marriages, she thinks. There are tourists even there. She stares out the window, reads signs: COTTON CANDY, DANONE YOGHURT, PERRIER. WE VACUUM-PACK FISH FOR AIR TRAVEL. CALIFORNIA SUN, LE CHATEAU BLANC, MAMMA'S PIZZERIA, EMPRESS OF THE EAST, KATAI SUSHI. Make it all feel like home. Alien, untrue.

Then, they cross into old Puerto Vallarta. Alice takes a deep breath. April is perfumed with familiarity: she and Morris arriving here twelve years ago. They've been married one day, and touch is so exquisite it hurts. His hands brush her arm, her shoulder, stroke her hair; his fingers wind around hers. She is intoxicated with love and desire. Everything's an aphrodisiac: the heat, the shimmering bodies, the music, the scent of tanning lotion, salt water, tortillas, *filets de pescado*. They had little back then, except each other.

"It was right here," Morris says, and looks at her, bewildered. The taxi has stopped in front of a mini shopping mall with a café on the second floor. "I told you we should have made reservations."

His voice is brittle, accusing.

"We never did before."

"This isn't then," he says with such finality she's not sure whether to press him, make him say what he really means. For once, couldn't they be honest with each other? No. It's too soon, or maybe too late. "Alice, for God's sake, let's just go to the Holiday Inn. It's not as if we can't afford it."

She looks up the street, at the old hotels that resemble the San Paolo — most of the Mexican ones do. "I want to stay in one of those," she says, stubborn. "Try the one up the street."

Finally in a room, while they unpack, Alice exclaims at the old fixtures, the bedspread, the table and chairs, the rusty refrigerator; calls them "quaint and charming."

"It's a pile of old junk," Morris says. "Stop romanticizing it. This is not Wonderland. We'd be a hell of a lot more comfortable in a new hotel and we wouldn't have to worry about sanitation." He sits gingerly at the edge of the bed as if it were a precipice. Alice waits. But he lies down and closes his eyes.

Alice continues to unpack, determined not to let him bait her. Maybe if he sleeps a bit, things will be different. She lies beside him, takes his hand, but he turns away from her.

Alice is not neurotic, helpless or dependent. While people her age were backpacking and finding themselves in Europe, Alice, with the help of a loan from her father, was busy pursuing a vision. By the time she and Morris met, she had paid her father back and owned (with the bank) her whimsical gift shop, *Alice in Wonderland*. Since then, Morris has bought into the store, and handles all the paperwork. Alice is the whimsy, Morris the practical.

She watches him sleep, the rise and fall of his chest, and for a moment she imagines herself falling down a well into a Wonderland where Morris catches her at the bottom like he did the night they drove, frenzied, to Stanley Park — eleven-thirty, full moon — parked the car and ran to the wolves' enclosures, because Alice wanted to witness their midnight howling. Which they didn't do, because the wolves were either hiding or sleeping. So Morris suggested it might be werewolves who bayed at the moon, and they both made monstrous faces and howled and bounded through the woods, until they reached the seawall. The tide was out and the moon's yellow finger split the water. Morris jumped onto the wet glistening stones, while Alice stepped on the wall and balanced three, four steps, before falling into Morris' arms and lips and laughter. Was it so long ago? Alice can't remember exactly.

They used to work well together, "building their future," they always said. Alice looks at Morris, at the sweep of his indifference to her. The future, she thinks suddenly, is an attitude. Enigmatic, undetermined, unnamed.

She knows he agreed to the holiday because he could see she was dangerously close to a hysterical showdown. Maybe in Mexico, she thinks, away from Susan, they will talk it out, resolve it. He must know she knows. Or does he really think her so naive?

She gets up quietly, showers and changes into a new dress. She's pretty, thin, has thick straight black hair that ends bluntly halfway down her back. Her eyes are blue and her skin olive. She's more than pretty, she's very striking. She's accustomed to appreciative looks, in the way beautiful women are. From everyone, she thinks, except

Morris, who has stopped seeing her. She has become familiar, comfortable, named. Alice. Wife. Nothing left to discover.

LATER, AFTER SUPPER AT LE CHÂTEAU BLANC, THEY FIND A Mexican bar. "One without gringos," Alice insists. Morris raises his eyebrows, but goes along, bar to bar, until they find one "too seedy for tourists," as he says. Alice doesn't care about the whys, she's trying to recreate an emotional state, solitude, the exclusivity of lovers in a crowd. Without distraction, they might fall in love again.

They drink together, bodies responding to the music. In the corner, a parade: strippers climb the postage-stamp stage and writhe to Latin rhythms. Clusters of men circle the stage, cheer, whoop, call them by name. In three songs, the women are naked and offering private orifices for public inspection. The men applaud, as if they've just been shown a magic trick. Some rise out of their seats, arms outstretched. The strippers deflect them with a flick of the hips, a twist of the ankle, a sweep of the hand — all as if it were part of the performance. Alice looks around at the groupings and couplings: against the bar, men engage in boisterous talk, words accented by slaps on each other's arms and backs; couples drink or talk or stare around the room hungrily; hookers and johns simulate intimacy; parties of young people toast one another; lovers speak with their eyes. *What do you think they're saying? Who do you think they are?* A safe examination of people's lives — anyone but theirs. The subtext hovers beneath the surface of her words — *Do you think they're having an affair?*— which Morris deftly ignores.

An hour, two. The tequila slides down easy. At the next table, a man sucks a hooker's nipple, his fingers kneading her white flesh.

When he lifts his head, the hooker takes a tissue from her purse, and carefully wipes his spittle off her breast before pushing it back into the bodice of her strapless dress. Alice laughs. There are boundaries everywhere.

Then, at the door, an entourage of soldiers. Alice focuses on the machine guns, imagines Elliot Ness, Valentine's Day. Instead, these soldiers nod and smile. A waiter leads them into the room, motioning *move back*. As they pass, here and there men stand and slightly bow.

"Who is it?" Alice asks.

Morris shrugs. "Some politician, likely. Who else would need a bloody army for protection?"

She sees him then. He's not a politician, but a military man, his eyes quick and observant. He has a stocky body and a broad face — almost ugly — yet she can't stop staring at him. He walks like a man who's accustomed to giving orders. She imagines his hands sanctioning unspeakable tortures. He lazily surveys the room, then settles at a nearby table and openly stares at her.

"From *El General*." The waiter nods in his direction when he sets down the drinks.

Alice moves closer to Morris. No tissue can wipe the general's stare from her body. There was a time when Morris would have sensed this, would have circled her shoulders with his arm, in the way men do when they're establishing territory.

"Genghis Khan's got his eye on you," Morris says.

"Shhhhhh." Alice sips her drink.

"Let's call him over." He raises his glass to the general.

"Morris, please —."

"He might as well stare at you here." Morris motions the general and his party to join them.

Soon the table is a clutter of empty shot glasses, and Alice laughs too often, too loudly, shaking her head so her hair fans like a hula skirt around her face.

The general has a way of smiling suddenly, quickly, which makes him appear boyish. Disarmed, Alice thinks. Or is he armed? He is not the kind of man she can easily decipher.

He leans into her. "Very pretty hair," he says, fingering it.

She feels his hand linger on her neck — let Morris see that other men find her attractive. She looks at him and shrugs.

What gets her is the pretense, the smiles and shrugs and laughter. The four of them last summer, she and Morris, Susan and Bill, on a camping holiday together — like forcible confinement. Yoho National Park in the Rockies. Did he really think she didn't wake up in the night, alone? Didn't see their flashlight beam disappear into the spiral railway tunnels? And in the morning, the four of them at breakfast, and Morris saying, "Couldn't sleep so I went for a walk." And Susan laughing. Alice, forced to smile. She could feel the shame creep up her body like ice water. And Bill, nodding a little too hard. Then later, Susan, her best friend, saying, "We ought to do this more often." And Alice, "Sure, a lot more often."

The general's English is good. He tells them he is in charge of the large prison nearby. "Many outlaws," he says, which makes Alice think of cheap Hollywood westerns. "You must be careful." He puts his arm on the back of her chair and whispers, "You Americans do not understand."

"Canadians," Alice says.

"*Sí*, Canadians too."

Alice imagines herself, gun in hand, holster hugging her hips. She and Susan, back-to-back, ready to begin ten paces while Morris cries, "Be careful. Be careful!"

THE GENERAL HAS AN ENDLESS REPERTOIRE OF PUNISHMENTS. "It is cause and effect," he says. "Vindication."

"Revenge doesn't change the original crime," Alice says.

"Maybe no." Historically, he tells her, the use of punishment is much older than the use of imprisonment. Public, too — humiliation being integral to the punishment.

While he talks, she glances at the machine guns around the table; thinks, he who has the biggest gun wins, or is it sins? The music pounds in her ears.

"I hear in America they have public executions." The general turns to Alice, his eyes penetrating. "In Texas, *sí*?"

"I wouldn't know," she says.

He sips his drink. It is his job, Alice thinks, while he defends the reputation of Mexican jails. This is a man whose ancestors established the Spanish Inquisition.

"American prisons," he says, "are like apartments."

Alice would like to contradict him — the loss of personal freedom, is he forgetting that? — but she is afraid. She would like to say: In *Canada*, we try to reform offenders, give them an opportunity to change. What good is punishment if they reoffend? She looks at Morris. He gives an imperceptible shake of the head.

Deterrence, Alice knows, does not work. It presumes that individuals act rationally in their own interests. That they will seek to escape the pain that punishment brings. She recalls the discussions — ground rules — when she and Morris were first together, the marriage vows they chose together — *I shall put no other before you;* the threats, *What God has put together, let no man put asunder. If it ever happens, I'll leave you.* I'll leave you, Alice thinks. What good is punishment without pain?

"You understand," the general says, "*el castigo,* the punishment, *la pena privativa de libertad*, the loss of freedom, is to keep the society from disintegrating."

"To ensure domestic tranquility," Alice says, and laughs. It's a phrase right out of the preamble to the U.S. Constitution.

"*Pérdon?*"

"Harmony in the family," Alice says. "Harmony." She sings a couple of notes.

The general doesn't get it, but he laughs with her. "Harmony. *Sí.*" His fingers snap another round to their table.

Morris has definitely upset their domestic tranquility. How to punish him? Drowning, stoning, hanging, beheading, burning at the stake, decapitation, drawing and quartering, electrocution, the gas chamber, lethal injection. Crucifixion. The possibilities endless. But how to make him love her the way he used to?

"I can show you the prison," the general says, abruptly, decisively. "Tomorrow."

Morris gives her a look, *no*. A Mexican jail is about the last thing she wants to see, but she says, "I'd love to come." Immediately, newspaper headlines flash through her brain: *Innocent Tourist Detained for 12 Years in Mexican Jail; 32-year-old Tortured Indefinitely; Husband and Lover Abandon Wife in Mexican Jail.*

The general and his entourage leave as swiftly as they entered. Alice and Morris find themselves facing each other and alone.

WHEN THEY GET UP, IT'S PAST ELEVEN AND THEY SHOWER quickly.

"I just don't know what got into you," Morris says, as if he were speaking to himself.

Alice looks at him in the mirror. She'd like to tell him there's a lot about her he doesn't know. But he turns away from her; goes into the bedroom to dress. They're committed now. She changes clothes three times. Morris flaps around her, asking questions in the air: *Should we bring our passports? IDs? Can we be arrested if we don't have them? How much money should we carry?*

In the cab, on the way to the Mexican jail, Morris stares out the window, his silence an accusation. Alice sits straight, her hand on her stomach, against the ID in the hidden wallet under her skirt. She feels a little queasy. In her purse, she finds two antacid tablets.

The prison looms in front of them like a fortress. *Abandon all hope ye who enter here ... Los desesperados.* Alice hears indistinguishable sounds — responses, perhaps, to tortures she can only imagine: whipping and flogging; branding with hot irons; amputation of ears, tongues, noses; eye gouging; deprivation of food and water; locking in a sweatbox ... She takes a deep breath, feeling hot and sticky inside the cab.

At the gatehouse, Morris gives the guard their names.

"*El General* no see you today. Important business. Tomorrow, you come."

BACK AT THE HOTEL, ALICE IS RELIEVED WHEN MORRIS INSISTS they pack quickly. They get in the cab; flee. "A small out-of-the-way place," Morris says. "We'll know it when we see it."

In the back seat, they are united in exhilaration, the sides of their bodies pressed against each other, hearts fluttering with danger. For a moment, Alice forgets her angst, the affair, Susan, and only the two of them remain, hurled into an adventure — each other, perhaps — like years ago, the night they got lost in Venice and neither of them spoke Italian and they wandered up and down skinny alleys, imagining shadows and footsteps following, and suddenly they recalled a movie just like this, and then they thought maybe this was the movie, and they had somehow been catapulted into it — by desire, perhaps — and, at any moment, they would turn a corner and find the man with the knife. Of course they laughed, nervous, terrified, and that night, back at the *pensione*, they made love, fierce and passionate.

Here, today, in Mexico ten years later, they lie on the bed without touching, memory a curse between them. When did it begin? Alice would like to ask him; to have him recount the details, leave nothing out. She remembers when his mother died, he told and retold stories about her, as if each telling was a way to examine, understand and sort the incident into his recollection. To order chaos. *What did I do? What could I have done?*

Their room is modest, basic — bed, dresser, basin, small mirror and a balcony facing an inner courtyard. Alice watches Morris at the mirror. He's meticulous — the careful shave, then dabs of aftershave; the brush wet just enough to coax the cowlick back; the clipper's snip snip snip of stray nose hair; the licked finger smoothing the eyebrows.

He used to do this secretly, used to emerge from the bathroom calling for her, awaiting her admiration. Handsome, narcissistic, Alice thinks. But he is not trying to impress her now, oblivious to her. She feels as if she is behind a one-way glass, a witness identifying a suspect at a police station. *Husband. Unfaithful.*

LATER, THERE IS A KNOCK AT THE DOOR. ALICE AND MORRIS look at each other. The knocking persists. Morris opens the door and the general is there, a mass of flowers in one hand, two bottles of tequila under his arms, a young woman at his side. "We have come to invite you to dinner," he says. "This is Aña. And this is Morris and his marvelous Alice."

"We've had dinner," Morris says, polite, his body blocking the doorway.

Behind him, Alice smooths the bedspread over the rumpled sheets. How did he find us? she wonders. Then she elbows Morris aside.

The general lays the flowers into her arms. Birds of paradise and frangipani. She breathes in their fragrance. *Lock him in an Iron Maiden; drag him behind wild horses; clamp him in a stock and pelt him with stones; throw him in front of a firing squad.*

The general sets one bottle on the dresser and opens the other. Aña produces four glasses from her large straw bag. Alice gives Morris a nudge, then she rotates the dial on the radio until the room pulsates with salsa rhythms. When the general has poured them all a drink, he insists they down it in one gulp. A tradition, he says, although Alice thinks he probably just made this up to get them drunk faster.

At first, they are all together, having a good time. The general sits in the one armchair, Aña on his lap; Alice and Morris settle on the bed. The general monologues his military achievements, describes both his city and country villas, recounts his travels, including the month he spent in Texas as a teenager.

ALICE IS NOT QUITE SURE HOW IT ALL HAPPENS, BUT BEFORE she knows it, one bottle is empty, and she is dancing outside on the balcony with the general. He is holding her too close; she can feel his erection against her stomach. Her nipples tingle; she feels flushed. Morris has not touched her since last summer. He has not touched *her*. Retribution, Alice thinks. A fuck for a fuck. How many nights would it take to even the score? The general kisses her throat. Let Morris suffer as much as she has. Through the looking glass, she suddenly sees Morris, dancing with Aña, her buttons undone to the waist. What good is punishment without pain? Alice's head feels enormous; she can't think. Have they always drunk this much? Those all-nighters back home — did they begin before or after Susan? Were they cause or effect? The general slips his hand under her T-shirt, squeezes her breast, still pressing her against him. Alice feels out of control, as if suddenly things have escalated beyond her boundaries. *When did it begin?*

"Let's go," the general murmurs in her ear. "We can go to my hotel."

"You don't understand," Alice says, her words slurring. She is leaning against the general, incapable even of pushing him away. "I don't do this. I'm married." The words sound empty, false, even to her own ears. She holds up her hand for him to see the wedding band, but it's not there — she must have left it on the basin.

"Your husband is busy," the general says.

"No." It takes enormous energy for her to stumble back into the room, to interrupt Morris' dance, to break through the alcoholic stupor. She fits herself into Aña's place, her heart against his, her lips on his neck. On the balcony, Aña joins the general.

When the second bottle is finally empty, the general and Aña move to the door. "*Mañana*," the general says before he leaves.

Alice and Morris fall into bed and make love furiously. Corporal punishment. Alice cries when it's over.

"MAYBE WE SHOULD SEPARATE FOR A WHILE," MORRIS SAYS IN the morning, while they pack quickly. He booked them an early flight home. "Give us both some space to work this out."

It isn't space I need, Alice thinks, her mind conjuring Siberia. In the ancient world, exile was considered equivalent to the death penalty because the individual would be cut off from home and family permanently. But the offender does not suffer alone. Suppose Morris' exile becomes a freedom? His pain, a joy? His temporariness, a permanence?

"Are you going to keep seeing her?"

"This isn't about Susan," Morris says.

Alice clicks her tongue and stares up into space, arms tight across her chest.

Morris continues to hurl things into the suitcase. "I know you're angry with me, Alice, and it's healthy for you to express your emotions," he says, his voice reasonable, rehearsed.

This is the part where he's supposed to say, "I love you. I'll never see her again. I can't live without you."This is the part where he's supposed to say, "I'm sorry." Contrition, remorse, reparation — conditions for parole.

But Morris continues to pack.

"What do I have to do?" Alice says. "Tell me what to do."

Outside, the air is humid and perfumed.

The French Woman

Each day now, Paula sinks into a canvas chair on the beach and furiously sketches The French Woman whose nationality she doesn't know, but whom she has, nevertheless, cast as French, because of the wide-brimmed hats, the long, colourful scarves, the eyelet off-the-shoulder blouses, the woman's sensual, unhurried walk, the knowing in her kohl-rimmed eyes. Before The French Woman materialized, Paula was carelessly happy. She arrived in Rimini a week before Ted to orient herself, to recline in a hammock in the *giardino* of her hotel and reread his letters — torrid words mingled with humid air.

She met Ted in Rome last summer, where she and her daughter, Andrea, escaped to after Paula's second divorce. Ted surfaced beside her one night in a bar, and seduced her with his crinkly blue eyes and offbeat wit. He recounted his stories — the plush red upholstery of the *Orient Express*, his teenage fear aboard a British Navy ship during the war, his excursions to Everest Base Camp and Mount Etna, his extreme bike tour through Canyonlands — and Paula fed him sporadic bites of her own past — her film-school scholarship, her Zen commune years, her trip to Goa where she met one of her former husbands, her car crash and near-death experience. Foreplay, really. On the eve of her flight home, they wrestled on the queen-sized bed of his hotel where, inexplicably, she reenacted a teenage virgin while he groped and cajoled and teased until, exhausted, he undressed, dove under the covers and launched into a frightening display of sleep apnea that compelled Paula to nudge him every few minutes. Finally, she stood up, tucked in her blouse and zipped up her pants, bewildered at herself, too embarrassed to return to her hotel, to walk through the lobby, though no one knew her. She cringed in the dark, regulating her breathing, trying to recall a time when she had not been ridiculous, when she had worn her nudity proudly and defiantly.

At dawn, she tiptoed into her room and found Andrea dressed and pacing. "How could you?" she kept saying, as if she were the mother and not nineteen. "He's old enough to be your father!"

"Don't exaggerate," Paula said, calm. "He's in very good shape."

"Yuk," Andrea said.

She has never told Andrea the truth, given how often she has delivered the when-I-was-your-age lecture: the good old braless, bare feet, flowing-gowns days; the free love in sleeping bags, at rock concerts, in communes; the demonstrations for equal pay, abortions, divorce settlements; etc.

"Oh Mom," Andrea always says. "Get with it."

Paula can't believe she spawned this conservative, prissy daughter. Andrea assumes her rights as if history did not exist. Just last week, Paula watched a rerun of *The Saint* in which a young woman who refused to cook and wash dishes was picked up and spanked like a child while she struggled and screamed. Later, of course, she cooked and cleaned and thanked Simon Templar and fell in love with him out of gratitude, even though he had to reject her in order to remain single and available to teach other *girls* lessons. Infantilized. Not that women in modern film are much different, Paula thinks. Ingenues, femme fatales or psychopaths. A variation on the Madonna/whore bit, give or take an axe.

Like most women, Paula evades these constrictions. She's forty-eight, divorced twice; a tall, large-boned woman with smooth skin, straight teeth and green eyes. She talks quickly, walks in long strides, and is impatient with fools. A technician in a photo lab, she develops portraits of grinning grads and wedding couples, of families whose scowls are expertly concealed beneath placid smiles.

During her film scholarship days, before she married and had Andrea, she had assumed she would become a brilliant director renowned for her original, meaningful films, for her quirky vivisections of middle-class values.

Today, the remains of that celluloid hunger are a series of amateurish, obvious, film-school shorts: four minutes of a hat on a Mexican beach, over which is heard a wartime broadcast of the battle on the beaches of Normandy; a pantomime/dance between a man dressed in a suit of armour and a woman wearing various domestic appliances; etc.

Two years ago, she began to paint. Each evening after supper, she watches films on video, and sketches the fleeting images. Later, she transforms them into paintings, aware that her depictions are four times removed. She probes art galleries; scrutinizes the exhibitions. *Exhibitions*. Like strip shows, or men in long raincoats. Andrea, who has been studying art history, looks at Paula's work and says, "Where are you in the painting?" Paula shrugs. "I'm painting the painting," she says, annoyed. On a wall of her room, Andrea has stencilled Fellini's words: *All art is autobiographical; the pearl is the oyster's autobiography*. Paula appreciates that: the precious as a consequence of irritation. She examines her own paintings, too, trying to see whether her autobiography is there, visible to the naked eye, to herself. Selective confession.

In the sketches, The French Woman wears a straw hat whose enormous brim flares to her shoulders. It is loosely fastened with a gauzy scarf that waterfalls over her ears, so that her face is a transparency of shadows. She could be the protagonist of a British period film: an aging lonely heart aching for romance, youth. But this is not Venice, it's Rimini in August, and the beach is teeming with Italian urbanites who flee to the seasides for *ferie*. She should have met Ted in Rome, Paula thinks, framing them in front of the Temple of the Vestal Virgins, or against the colonnade of St. Peter's, faces airbrushed smooth. But it's better this way. New territory. She rode the train from Bologna so she could cross the Rubicon, stride toward something dangerous. Gave her a surge of power, although she knows she won't be causing any civil war.

When husband #1 left, Paula abandoned the West Coast, headed into a hearth of darkness, a sweat lodge in a small Alberta town.

Spiritual healing. Sixteen strangers orbiting a pit stacked with forty-two incandescent rocks, the lodge sealed from the outside. Paula crouched, naked under a long T-shirt, clutching a towel, terrified. The medicine man began to chant and fling cupfuls of water into the pit. Paula folded the towel over her nose and mouth, gasping at each new burst of steam, until her voice became a plaintive, desperate wail. Lemongrass swirled in the air, and Paula hallucinated flickering lights — fugitive ghosts from Dante's Inferno. What she recalls most, even now, is the hysterical certainty that she would suffocate.

Paula squints at her watch. An hour till Ted arrives. The thought of seeing him catches in her throat like a fishbone.

Six months since her last panic attack. February 14th. She was at the Stanley Theatre, on Singles Night, when all those expectant faces and famished smiles triggered the smell of sweet grass. The black of the lobby enveloped her, the air blazed in her lungs. Later, Andrea told her it was Freudian: *anxiety arises when instinctual aggressive or sexual drives threaten to lead a person to behave unacceptably, and that it acts as a signal that triggers defensive action to repress or redirect these drives.* Paula scoffed. She does not consider herself sexually repressed; she has a trunkful of sexual escapades as proof, even though these predate her marriages. Now, suddenly single in her forties, she's afraid that sensuality may be perceived as vulgarity; she's afraid to resemble The French Woman who parades her pretty boys in tight jeans and slicked-back hair as if they were trophies.

WHEN THE KNOCK COMES, SHE'S IN HER ROOM CHANGING, this time into an emerald silk chemise and pants and the strappy sandals she bought yesterday. She feels attractive and *European.*

"You must be Paula." The man extends his hand. "I'm Jason. A friend of Ted's." He is about her age, a nondescript man with brown doe eyes.

"Where's Ted?" she asks. "Is he all right?"

"Could we go somewhere and talk?" He shifts his weight from foot to foot.

She shrugs, then leads him downstairs to the outdoor lounge. "Is Ted all right?" she asks again, once they're seated.

"Not exactly," Jason says, then explains that Ted died eight months ago, a victim of a hit-and-run. "It was instantaneous. He didn't suffer," he says as if this makes it okay.

Paula frowns. She received a letter from Ted two weeks ago. "Is this some kind of joke?" She feels oddly detached from the news, as if Ted were a minor character in a film she hasn't seen. She begins to stand up.

"No. Please." He waves her back into her seat. "I know it sounds crazy. I'll explain everything." He tells her that *he* has written all the letters. "At first, Ted asked me if I'd do it. He wasn't good with words ... and ..."

Paula's cheeks flush; her chest constricts. She inhales slowly and deliberately. She's surprised, of course, that the Ted she has been writing to does not exist, never existed. But to think that this Jason, this *stranger* has been eavesdropping on her private thoughts, that he has slithered his way into her familiarity. She feels betrayed. She feels *instinctual aggressive drive*. "How could you do such a thing?" she says. "And to ask me to meet you here ..." She doesn't know whether to scream or punch him.

"Look. I didn't see the harm. People meet through the Personals and through the internet. I'm the one you've been writing to. You know me a lot better than you ever knew Ted."

"But you pretended you were someone else. You deliberately deceived me!"

They stare at each other for a moment, and Paula is mortified she said that. Why couldn't she have said, "You jerk," or "Fuck you," instead of sounding like the wronged woman in a 1950s western, where the rogue swaggers out of a Marlboro ad — a smudge on his cheek and a twinkle in his eye — and the woman is blonde and petite, and wears virginal cotton dresses and wide belts. And he's worldly and sophisticated, and she's pure and naive and, of course, she forgives him whatever he's done, but only after she makes him suffer and grovel and kill the antagonist in a brilliant show of courage. Screw that, Paula thinks, and laughs. Jason hesitates a moment, then he, too, laughs. "Now what?" she says.

"OH, POOR MOM," ANDREA WAILS ACROSS THE ATLANTIC WHEN Paula tells her the latest. "Did you call the police immediately?"

Paula explains that no, she didn't call the police nor does she intend to. In fact, later, she and Jason are going dining and dancing.

"What if he's a serial killer, or a pervert? Mother, have you gone mad?"

"Look," Paula says. "If I go missing, you've got a sample of his handwriting in the letters."

If Paula had been an actress of her mother's generation, she would have been cast in Joan Crawford roles. This is her personal myth, what she has always told Andrea, who has metamorphosed into an insufferable little prude since Paula became single again.

Suddenly, she is embarrassed by Paula's "flaky artsy-fartsy" friends, by their vintage clothes and attitudes, by the Indian throws and the beaded curtains. She is embarrassed by the purple of the bathroom wall, the yellow retro couch, the framed Beatles record jackets, by anything to do with Paula. If Paula could turn the whole house white and herself invisible, she might be acceptable to Andrea. She hangs up, happy to be on another continent.

Outside on the beach, The French Woman settles on her blanket, as she does every afternoon. She speaks to no one except the gypsies who return day after day with wooden cases full of necklaces, bracelets and rings in semiprecious stones, silver, gold. Paula captures them in her sketchbook: the gypsies distinct, alien and exotic, with their black eyes and hair, their ringed fingers, their ankle bracelets; The French Woman, a swirl of gauze and hats. The real gypsies are not as romantic — threadbare clothes, hungry eyes, gestures aggressive and hostile. When she arrived, the hotel concierge told her to be cautious, to zip her cash in a money belt and not to speak to the gypsies, who "will take advantage of the slightest confidence." Well, The French Woman appears at ease. She fills her large straw bag with trinkets. Paula tapes the sketches and watercolours to the walls of her room.

JASON HAS RESERVED A TABLE IN THE INNER COURTYARD OF AN elegant restaurant. They sit among magenta bougainvillaea and tall, pink geraniums. He orders a bottle of wine, and begins his monologue. Paula extends her face into multiple grimaces of interest. The letters she wrote were to Ted, not to this man who, although they are practically strangers, drags his heavy trunk between them, opens the lid and unleashes his miserable stories. There's something detestable about a man who abridges his past to fit into a three-course dinner, a man who tells all at once, as if he does not believe in mystery. Too much exposition, Paula thinks, like TV. She's sick of soap operas; sick of masquerading as the sympathetic audience; sick of listening to this or that wife's shortcomings, this or that mother's overpossessiveness, this or that father's absence, this or that — fill in the blanks — "poor me" story. "Get on with it," she'd like to shout at them all. "Grow up!" She prefers older men because their future is more urgent with worries: retirement, deteriorating health, death. They distill their pasts into intense adventures, cast themselves as romantic leads.

When they arrive back at the hotel, it's nearly midnight — early in Rimini, in Italy, in August — when many families sit down to dinner and lovers dress for nightclubs. Jason is gasping and wheezing; every few steps, he draws on a puffer. "It's the smoke," he tells her. "These Italians don't seem to care about their health." She's limping along beside him, one sandal on, the other dangling from her fingers. The heel broke off in one of the alleys. What a picture they must make, Paula thinks, when they reach the hotel and she sees The French Woman framed in a cluster of dazzling young people, laughing as if she had not a care in the world. She's all in white — a crinkle-cotton see-through dress, gathered at the back by a criss-cross of cotton rope in which coins and bells and rings are braided. Perhaps it's the way she flips her hair away from her face, or the scarlet lips that make Paula hurry past, her chest a vacuum of longing. She helps Jason up the stairs to his room.

He flops into a chair, and undoes the buttons of his shirt. Paula gazes out the window, at The French Woman, who swings her hips like a runway model, who flips her hand at the wrist, this way and that, as if she were a celebrity, saluting. Paula wants to phone Andrea right now to tell her that on a deathbed, nobody ever wished to have had less sex, to have been more prudent, more proper.

"I'm a lot better," Jason says. "I can never go to nightclubs at home either."

Paula wonders where else he can't or won't go, how else he distances himself from life. "Tell me something good about a relationship you've had," she says.

He looks startled, frowns. "What do you mean?"

She raises her eyebrows at him. What she'd like to ask is: What do you do on Sundays? Do you own any paintings? Have you been inside the catacombs? Instead, she shakes her head. "Is this the part where we sleep together?" she says.

And now it is his turn to go to the window: it's the asthma, of course, or the medication. He hasn't slept with a woman in years. But he's sure, if she'll just bear with him, it'll be different this time. She freeze-frames for a moment, thinking this is the epiphany in the movie where the two pathetic lonely hearts transcend their inadequacies and advance toward spiritual redemption. She can almost hear the elevator music, see sentimental tears spring forth, like acid rain.

She turns and flees the room, the hotel, the man. In moments, she's running down streets, barefoot, pursuing instinct until she comes to a sign, La Dolce Vita, pointing to a crooked alley. All around, the outdoor cafés are brimming with elegance, vitality.

Paula feels dowdy, weighed down. She wonders if Jason is still wheezing in his room, or if he is in a taxi bound for the train station. She wonders what story he will tell about her.

She buys a pack of cigarettes from an outdoor vendor and smokes two, before entering. The bar is a tribute to Fellini, who was born here. On the walls are framed stills from his films — his autobiography, a mixture of beauty and grotesque. Paula stands in a corner and watches the floor show through a filter of smoke, the heat oppressive. She wills herself back in time, into a black-and-white film — she is Marilyn Monroe, perhaps, or Jane Russell on a cruise, singing "A kiss on the cheek might be quite Continental ..." The men form a girdle of admiration. Paula watches their faces, the gestures, envious of their rehearsed love.

Warm breath. A young man murmurs in her ear, "*La signora* is alone? Perhaps *La signora* is looking for an English student?"

She shakes her head. Her chest constricts and her heart begins to pound. It is as if the oxygen has been sucked out of the room, her lungs seared with shame. She pushes past the young man, into the night air, the heat, into a circle of gypsy children who smother her with their small clutching hands, their jingly jewellery.

"Give money." A young boy, perhaps seven or eight, touches her arm.

Paula recoils, shakes her head.

"Give money now." The children tug at Paula's clothes, so she has to turn this way and that to avoid them. Her moneybelt is flat against her stomach. She tries to jostle past them.

The boy reaches out once more, grabs Paula's arm. "You give money," he says.

Paula elbows him aside, panting. The children move back. The young boy's eyes narrow. He steps forward and spits in Paula's face.

For a moment, neither of them moves, then the gypsy children scatter and disappear before Paula can react. She wipes off the spit and runs back to the hotel, her heart hammering.

Jason's goodbye note is under her door, and she knows she, too, should board a train, a plane, get back to something familiar. Her room is sweltering, so she chain-smokes in the open landing, watching the street, vaguely aware that she's waiting for The French Woman. She stubs out her cigarette when she sees her come up the stairs.

"*Buona sera*," she says.

The French Woman looks startled, as if it never occurred to her that other people are registered here. Her partner is hardly more than a boy — eighteen, nineteen. He is a step behind her, his hands at either side of her waist. She turns to him, then smiles at Paula. They both nod as they pass.

Paula remains seated in darkness. She hears them settle outside, on the floor above; the clink of glasses, the murmur of voices, the bursts of laughter. What could they possibly be saying? The French Woman whispering and leaning forward in that low-cut dress, as if she thinks she's twenty and not fifty and counting. Tomorrow, Paula thinks, she'll get on the first train back to Bologna, then see if she can change her flight home. She'll move to California, sell watercolours in Newport Beach, get a facelift, buy leisure wear, marry a wealthy banker and live happily ever after. She pours herself a drink, and smokes five more cigarettes.

Finally, when the phosphorescent face of her watch reads 3:26 a.m., everything is quiet, everyone in bed. She wonders if Ted is really dead, if gypsies sleep. She wonders about The French Woman upstairs. What is she back home? A librarian? A bookkeeper? A spinster nursing an ill parent? Something repressed and constricting. Paula can't imagine The French Woman acting like this in her hometown, in her life. She stubs out the last cigarette in her pack. Picks up her glass and stands. But instead of going to her room, she sets the glass down and goes up to the next landing. In the darkness, she can see the table, the silhouettes of tumblers, a Chianti bottle. Still life. Herself once, twice removed.

She leans against the door, breathless, adrenaline pumping through her veins. She's in a foreign city in the middle of the night, surrounded by The French Woman, by the deafening jingle of bracelets and bells, closing in.

Public Relations

B arra de Navidad, Mexico. It's 11:23 on New Year's Eve
1996, and while the Zapatista National Liberation Army
drafts its Declaration of War and Revolutionary Laws,
Magda is tramping around in a gang of seven, looking for some
action. No one's made a reservation — a fact Magda thinks must
be significant: an embodiment, perhaps, of vice or virtue.

"There's got to be a nightclub somewhere," Colin says. He runs
his fingers along Magda's inner arm, causing small delicious shivers. He's an out-of-work actor who's been fawning over her all day.

"Or a nice lounge," Gavin says, timid. He's seventy, old enough
to be their dad and then some. Beef-jerky skin, thick white hair,
impenetrable eyes.

"It'd be nice to dance," Steve says. He and Carianne are celebrating their twentieth anniversary. The other two, Julie and Lee, are newlyweds.

Over the last week, they've been bonding and now are inseparable, their lives slowly leaking out. While Magda has managed not to spill any of hers, Gavin has been drenching them with his, which, to Magda, sounds like a soft-focus commercial for a seniors' time-share: he's fit, independent; he cared for his wife until she died of cancer three years ago; he sold his house and now gypsies up and down Mexico — a few months here, a few there; he has had a successful career as a PR troubleshooter (could make an oil spill sound like salad dressing); and he is well known and liked by everyone here — staff and guests. Magda thinks there's something unnatural about a man who, in his first week at a new hotel, befriends 104 people.

Ironically, all this goodwill does not extend to his own family: Gavin speaks bitterly about his daughter — a sad story, which Magda suspects is a sympathy plea.

"What could I do?" Gavin says, staring at Magda. "Sixteen years old and decides to be a singer." He shakes his head. "Well, I told her: Missy, you can choose my way or the highway."

His way was to finish high school, go to college, get a job, a car, a husband, a house, etc. and live happily ever after. His daughter chose the highway. Joined a band, and sat at the back of beat-up Econoline vans, among instruments and suitcases and beer bottles, hurtling toward an uncertain future as a musician.

This is Magda's version of the story so, when Gavin finishes, she doesn't have the appropriate reaction. He's expecting a shake of the head, *Poor Gavin*. Magda wants to know what instrument his daughter plays. What kind of music does she sing? What's her vocal range? All these, Gavin answers with a shrug. He's never heard her sing or play. Magda's hand tingles — slap anticipation.

More and more, recently, Magda has had to resist the overwhelming urge to slap someone. She has appropriated this urge from late-night movies, where the slap is instant retribution. *You've insulted me,* it says, *and now we're even.* Slap the offenders and skip the therapists. A simplistic restoration of balance. Back home, once she began to fantasize practical applications, the list grew dangerously: the man honking in the alley at 6 a.m., the truck driver gearing down in front of her house, the Jehovah's Witnesses on Sunday mornings, the insolent checkout clerk at Safeway, the woman next door pining over some loser, the loser himself, the guitar player (Bruce) when he arrived late for dinner, and of course, herself, in the bathroom, before and after sex and, most of all, during the meaningless sex it had become. Slap! Slap! Slap! Her relationships with men, an archetype of public ease and private dis-ease. Get a life, girl, she told herself. Break the cycle. Booked the next flight into Puerto Vallarta, then hopped a bus, and here she is, urges and all, in Barra de Navidad. Christmas spit.

Gavin's been dropping his daughter's story piecemeal all week, like an advertisement for a new car. *K. Wait for it — K. K is coming.* He treats everyone as he may have treated his clients. Courteous, thoughtful. The perfect PR Man, *in the business of inducing the public to have understanding for and goodwill toward him.* Slap. Magda, who is very suspicious of benevolence, has watched him work a room: he offers a slice of special bread he found yesterday, a particularly sweet piece of watermelon, a glass of wine, a candle, a smile, an anything-I-can-do-for-you. Everyone loves him. Everyone but his daughter, of whom Gavin seems to have no recollection except as a truant, a fugitive, a deserter.

"A singer," he says, grimacing an acrid taste.

What sparks all this discussion/confession is that on the street, they find a scraggly group of expatriates playing guitar and singing corny campground songs — the way tourists do when they're away from home and feeling sentimental. They join in, creating what never was: "Home, home on the range ... where seldom is heard a disparaging word ..."

Perhaps it's the distance in the words, Magda thinks. Perhaps Gavin is listening to another time and place, another campground where he and his family are gathered around a fire — his daughter, eight, in her long flannel nightie, her voice a sweet soprano, her arms outstretched. His wife puts her hand on his arm, smiles. Perhaps the power of the child's voice or the melody that penetrates his heart frightens him. Perhaps he hears her escape years later, her spirit elsewhere.

So, when they realize Magda's a singer, someone asks her to do a number and she does. Music gets to everyone, even Gavin. At the end of the song, he's beaming at her. "Gosh," he says.

THAT FIRST NIGHT WHEN GAVIN'S DAUGHTER LEFT, SHE GOT on a bus and rode it round a city loop until the bus driver parked behind a chain-link fence. He turned a crank above him and scrolled through a sequence of bus names — *Granville, Hastings, Victoria, Kootenay Loop* — stopped at that morning's designation.

She had watched him do this all night; watched the bus change name, according to location. An illusion — one bus masquerading as many. It made her think

- she could be a chameleon (years later, on stage, she wore costumes and stage names);
- about the power of words;
- how by renaming something, you could change the object itself;
- daughter, stranger.

The bus driver motioned her out with a shake of the head — by now, they'd been trading stories for several hours — and took her home to the apartment he shared with his wife and small baby. The hardest part was not calling: Dear Mom, I am not lost, kidnapped, raped, or dead.

Her father, she was certain, would be out in his car, cruising around, looking for her ... where? *My way or the highway*. For years she rode a bus round the city, and each time the driver turned the crank, she renamed herself: daughter, teen, runaway, woman, musician.

A SUCCESSION OF PLANES THUNDERS ACROSS THE SKY. MAGDA looks up into the black, unwilling to mouth the words. "Charters," someone says, nervous. For days now, they've heard rumours about an uprising of Mayan Indians and other poor farmers in Chiapas. (MEXICAN BROTHERS AND SISTERS: *We are the product of 500 years of struggle* ...) The Mexican government has sent in armed persuasion. *My way or the highway*. One form of death for another. Magda stares at Gavin. He's frowning too. She shakes her head. Don't think about it. Slap. It's New Year's Eve, Colin's arm circles her waist, and on they go, down the street, Gavin still telling his story.

At first, when Gavin's wife, Beth, was diagnosed with cancer, Gavin refused to believe it. He didn't say so, naturally, not to Beth. But in his head, a voice kept saying: It's all a mistake. "We'll find another doctor," he told her, caught in his own PR, trying to control not the cancer — he knew this would be futile — but the naming of it, as if the word itself could validate it, make it real. *Goodthink.* Eliminate undesirable words. Governments did it all the time, renamed the negatives to positives: unemployment insurance to Employment Insurance; civilian deaths to Collateral Damage; contraception to Family Planning. Naturally, every new doctor said "cancer," until Beth made Gavin say it too, being exhausted by test after test. PR could control the public mind, but it could not control Beth's body.

In the music business, Magda thinks, to do PR, means:

- drink with customers;
- talk to people she'd rather not know;
- attend tedious parties;
- stroke a clubowner's ego; etc.

In short, do something she doesn't want to do. Commercial persuasion. Sometimes she makes a joke of it, an explanation, a justification for last night's pickup: "Just doing PR," she tells a girlfriend.

PR: public relations, personal revulsion.

THREE MINUTES TO MIDNIGHT, THEY RUN THROUGH A HOTEL lobby to the beach. Take off their shoes and look up. For now, the sky is only full of stars. (In the Lacandona Jungle, the Zapatistas prepare their Declaration of War: TODAY WE SAY ENOUGH IS ENOUGH! ...) The surf explodes on a ledge and a salt tongue licks higher and higher up the shoreline, over Magda's feet and ankles, up the beach. Tepid water, calm and harmless until it begins to recede. They all run to dry sand at the first insinuation of the riptide.

At midnight, fireworks ignite the sky, and everyone kisses. Colin waits to be last, then pulls Magda against him, his hand in the small of her back, and thrusts his tongue into her mouth. In the darkness, while the others shout "Happy New Year!" Magda returns the kiss, then pushes him away, embarrassed, when she realizes Gavin is watching.

"Let's get a drink," she says, deliberately casual, although she needn't be, because it's dark and New Year's and everyone is brimming with unfulfilled desire. She puts on her shoes and forges a path to the nearest bar.

GAVIN GLAD-HANDS HIMSELF INTO A SEAT BESIDE HER. "YOU ever been married?" he asks when their drinks arrive, as if they've been discussing this all along.

"No. Never had time," Magda says. Too many bands, cities, men. Human contact, a revolving door of skin, scent and darkness. Instinctual, necessary. She can't fall in love with her eyes closed. "But I'm not alone," she adds.

"Oh." The tone of his voice tells her that he does not understand.

"Extramarital sex," Magda says, and laughs.

Gavin's daughter sent postcards to her mother, sometimes a letter, from a medley of towns and cities and countries. She joined and left this band and that band, in the way musicians do. Transient. Unencumbered. Detached. The promo photos always showed her smiling. Beth filed them all in a recipe box, first chronologically, then by provinces and states, and finally by countries. Now and then, she left them out, hoping Gavin would read them.

"And did you?" Magda asks.

"Never."

Soon, they run out of things to do. It's 2:00 a.m. Nothing open. They head for the bonfires on the beach, drag out their plastic chairs and table, a pitcher of margaritas and they're ready. Magda sings a couple of songs; Carianne and Julie do the macarena; Colin performs the opening monologue of an obscure play; Lee and Steve do a charade of two men washing an elephant; Gavin claps, ever smiling, and watches them all and finally, Magda knows there's no escaping it: they want to know why a forty-year-old woman would take a two-week Mexican vacation alone.

She tells them she's *recuperating*, knowing full well that this is a word that chokes questions and launches the imagination. "A miracle," she begins. "A few bruises and scrapes, headaches for a week. Nothing ten days in bed couldn't cure." Pressed for details, she tells them about the highway, the slick of oil and rain. Fire. Bodies side by side on the shoulder — like archeological finds, tagged and numbered. Sirens. Fire trucks. Ambulances. Hoses thick like pythons, quivering with pressure. The water sprays in the glare of red and blue lights circling — like a fantastic Vegas show. Fear, a large vacuum sucking up all other emotions. Four dead. Three in serious condition. And she, unharmed.

What she doesn't tell them is that all this is conjured from a trash TV movie she saw last week in the middle of the night. What she doesn't tell them is that her band broke up and along with it, her so-called relationship with Bruce, the guitar player. Broke up.

Like a frozen river in spring. Shattered into ice floes drifting to uncertain destinations. Uncertain, maybe, but predictable. What she doesn't tell them is that there's no one to care if she lives or dies, that her mother's dead and that she has been estranged from her father for twenty-four years.

Everyone's stunned after her story and Magda almost feels guilty, seeing their genuine emotion. She stares at the sea; focuses on the explosions of breakers on the shore, on the dangerous, invisible undertow.

"*Aaamaaaziiing Grace,*" she begins to sing, "*hooow sweet the sound, that saaaaved aaa wretch liiike meeeeee ...*" Her voice rises in blue tones, the music forcing her own emotions to the surface.

"My wife died slowly," Gavin says suddenly, as if he's in the middle of a story. "Eleven months of pain."

Magda continues to sing, aware that music erases boundaries. His voiceover fills the pauses between her lines. "*Iiii once waaas lost, buuut now I'm found ...*"

"Every day," he says, "for eleven months, she asked if there was a letter from our daughter."

"*... Waaas blind, buut now I seeeee ...*"

"Beth died," he says, "longing for her daughter."

And suddenly it feels like night, cold and silent. Magda stops singing and Carianne reaches out and pats Gavin's arm. "That's so sad," she murmurs.

"Why didn't you tell your daughter?" Magda leans forward in her chair.

Gavin shakes his head. "I didn't know where she was."

"You must have had some idea," Magda insists, her throat tight.

"An old address? She had to live somewhere."

"Let's go wish the kids Happy New Year," Steve says, nudging Carianne. "It must be midnight at home by now."

He's embarrassed, Magda thinks, by her probing the details of Gavin's personal life. She knots her shawl around her shoulders. Gavin stares into the black. Colin begins to gather glasses. Julie and Lee turn to each other and kiss. They're all anxious to flee. The difference between "flee" and "feel" is in the placement of the *l*, Magda thinks. Love? Lust? Life? They get up, gather their chairs and stampede toward the hotel.

"I wrote her a letter," Gavin says, his voice crisp, "after my wife died."

They pause, polite, yet anxious not to hear more.

"I told her of the suffering she caused." He walks past the swimming pool before they have a chance to comment, and up the stairs to his room.

Colin nods to Magda. "You want to go for a swim?"

She knows he means a fuck. The others whisper good night.

"Why not?" she says.

THE NEXT MORNING, MAGDA GETS UP EARLY AND HOPS ON THE first bus to anywhere. Colin goes along for the ride. She sits by the window and stares at the buildings, which quickly metamorphose into banana plantations and mango groves and coconut palms. Colin pulls out his videocam and starts shooting. He could be making a commercial for FiestaWest Holidays. Keep the camera pointed up, away from the roadside shanties and burning garbage. Controlled exposure. Magda thinks about last night, glad Colin was there to distract her. She wonders if Gavin is sequestered in his room, embarrassed, perhaps.

"He never finished the story," she tells Colin. "He left out his daughter's reaction."

"That's not the point," Colin says. "We're supposed to feel sorry for Gavin."

"Who does he think he is?" Magda says.

(On the balcony of the Municipal Presidential Palace in San Cristobal, Sub-commander Marcos answers questions after reading the Declaration of War:

Question: Why are some of you masked and others are not, although you are all from the same movement?

Marcos: ... we have to watch out for protagonism, in other words, that people do not promote themselves too much.)

LATER, MAGDA AND COLIN WALK THROUGH CIHUATLÁN, IN search of an open restaurant. It's past 1:00 p.m., and everything's already closed for siesta. The sidewalks are uneven, potholed, treacherous. Colin takes her hand, then drops it when he sees up ahead, in front of a dilapidated shack, a tiny girl — four or five perhaps — seated on the sidewalk, legs straight out in front of her. She is wearing a handmade jumper and is shoeless. Although the videocam whirs, she does not look up when they pass, because she is concentrating on the glossy brochure on her lap. Four pages of Slumber Party Barbie, Glitter Barbie, Tropical Splash Barbie, Shopping Barbie, Tattoo Barbie, for God's sake, impeccable Barbie, etc. — fresh and incongruous in the heat and dust.

"Surely this is advertising gone rampant," Magda says to Gavin later, when they're all together at sunset. Of course, no one has mentioned last night.

"It's just information," Gavin says. "You've got to let some people know."

"And what good is that going to do?" Magda suppresses a slap. Gavin shrugs.

"You never bought Barbies for your daughter," Magda says.

"She never wanted one," Gavin says, eyes unflinching.

What she did ask for were records and musical instruments and sheet music and piano lessons. She began to seriously use the word "musician" soon after her fourteenth birthday. Gavin tried various techniques of persuasion: he outlined her entire life in negatives if she chose this career:

• she would have no hope of good money and better jobs;

• no security against the hazards of old age and illness; and

• no social advancement.

When his daughter didn't react, Gavin added:

• less comfort;

• decreased enjoyment;

• degenerate appearance; and

• deteriorating health.

His daughter laughed. "You're not trying to sell me toothpaste, Dad. There's no point to your *ballyhoo, hoopla, hype, puffery, squib.*" She said these slowly, mocking him, having watched him plan campaigns, toy with words and phrases into the night.

She had been singing in the school choir for years (which Gavin considered frivolous but respectable), but recently, had formed a rock band with four teenagers (all boys — which Gavin did not consider respectable). They met after school and on weekends (Beth said things like, "It keeps her out of trouble.") Gavin would not even consider letting them rehearse in the basement. He resorted to the fundamental technique: repetition. Followed her around the house in negatives. For two more years she stood it. Avoidance is like Chinese opera — put on a mask and costume and acrobat your way around obstructions. Tumble and roll and twist and turn.

ALL WEEK, DAILY, THE PLANES. THE MEXICAN ARMY HAS surrounded the city of San Cristobal. The hospital in nearby Comitan is flooded with casualties and the press is excluded from the area. (WE, THE MEN AND WOMEN, FULL AND FREE, ARE CONSCIOUS THAT THE WAR THAT WE HAVE DECLARED IS OUR LAST RESORT, BUT ALSO A JUST ONE ...) The planes glint in the afternoon sun; rumble past in the middle of the night. "Charters," people say. Today, on the front page of the Mexican newspaper, a photo of six armed Zapatistas.

"Talk about PR," Magda says. "There's a fucking army down there, and all we see is this." She flings the newspaper on the table.

Gavin frowns. She's not sure which word he finds objectionable, "fucking" or "PR."

"Everyone's looking to bitch at something," Colin says. He shakes suncreen out of a bottle, and dabs it on his nose.

"Yeah, sure," Magda says. "The Zapatistas have no land, no work, no health care, no education —."

"They've got guns," Julie says.

"The Zapatistas are not violent; they are *resisting* violence." Magda shakes her head.

Gavin picks up the paper and studies the photo for a moment. "Don't you understand? It's PR. The government has to justify why it's attacking its own people."

Even armies have PR departments, Magda thinks. Douglas MacArthur — the American general who commanded the Allied troops in the Pacific during WWII, supervised the postwar occupation of Japan, led U.N. forces during the Korean War, toured the Orient as his father's aide, and served as aide to President Theodore Roosevelt — was the army's first Public Relations Officer. PRO.

PRO: a professional, a public relations officer, a prostitute.

ON THE AFTERNOON OF THE DAY COLIN LEAVES, THEY ARE ALL assembled in the lobby. They've had the Last Breakfast, the Last Lunch, the Last Beach Walk; everything they've done together, they called the "Last …" In his room, this morning, Colin scribbled his phone number on the back of his room receipt and handed it to Magda. She pressed it back into his hand. "Last Tango," she said. When the taxi arrives, they help with the luggage, then stand together and wave until the taxi disappears in the dust. On the beach, they settle on deck chairs and anxiously chatter to neutralize the gloom, the imbalance created by Colin's departure.

"Look at that," Gavin says, looking at the water. "Calm as can be. Anybody for a swim?"

Everyone declines. On this beach, waves suddenly rise like enraged sea monsters — otherworldly gods or demons — trying to come ashore. And if they break on you, you could be lucky and only fracture an arm or a leg. Or you could drown. Already in the past two months, three people have drowned.

This is the part you never see in the brochures — the photos capture the trademark, those *symbols of reliability and value*: the aquamarine of a calm sea, the brilliant lozenges of sun on the ripples, the white sand, the palms, the lovers walking eternally hand in hand on the edge of paradise. Beyond the glossy, the photographer snaps shut the camera case, folds the tripod, and labels this film "Barra de Navidad." It's hard to distinguish one beach from another. The two models slip into their shorts and bicker over where to stop for lunch. They all pile into the Land Rover and head for the nearest American hotel.

Gavin looks at Magda, questioning.

"Let's do a few laps in the pool, instead," she says.

"Come on. It's fine. Not a wave for miles." He goes in, quickly swims past the ledge — that border between shallow and depth. She follows into the warm water, into that glossy photo. Lies on her back and stares up at the clear blue sky, the occasional pelican overhead. When she lifts her head and looks at the shore, everyone waves. And suddenly, she senses danger, turns and sees a wall of water. She dives into its centre, then comes up for air. The wave batters the shore, then ebbs, creating an undertow. Magda looks for Gavin. He is a little too close to the ledge, caught in the purgatory where the wave breaks then sucks. He's scrambling forward.

"Gavin!" she shouts. "Don't try to go in. Come further out."

He turns to her, confused. A new wall of water approaches.

"Dive under," she says and does so herself. When she resurfaces, she can see Gavin trying to beat the wave to shore. It pummels him, grinding him down, under. She swims closer, careful to stay away from the ledge herself. Drowning is that easy. They don't say that in the guidebooks.

Gavin surfaces, his face red, his hair a tangle of sand. The ocean drags him out.

"Don't fight it!" Magda yells. "Come on out with it."

He listens then, floats out toward her. She prays he won't panic and drown them both. She swims to meet him, becomes the barrier he leans against … *Magda … your mother …* The letter dissolves between them. Gavin is winded, his mouth open and gasping. Magda looks to shore, sees Julie snap a Polaroid photo, unaware of their predicament.

"It's all right," she says to him, to herself. "You just float. I'm going to hold your head up and swim out a little. I've got you. It's all right." She thinks, suddenly, that they might drown just as the Polaroid develops on shore. They will look like father and daughter, heads close together.

Gavin continues to gasp, but does as she says, his eyes trusting. "My daughter …" he begins, between gasps.

"Save your energy," she says. "You're going to need it going in."

"You don't understand," Gavin says.

Magda counts waves as they go past and rise into breakers. Four. Every seven or so, there's a lull. At least, that's the myth. She can't keep them out here forever. Five. They should try to go in on the seventh. "You've got to help me now," she tells him. "When I say, you start swimming in with me. I'll be right beside you."

She counts till the right moment, then says, "Now!" They catch the crest and ride the wave as it rises. Gavin sputters beside her, taking in water.

"I lied," he says. "I had your address all along. I wanted to punish you."

Magda grabs his arm and holds on while the wave snakes through them like an electric current and smashes into shore. "Now!" she says. "Run in." Together, they push forward, against the powerful undertow, feet burrowing in sand.

The others come running and drag them onto the beach. Both Gavin and Magda are panting and exhausted. Magda's thoughts are a series of slaps.

When she has her breathing more in control, she looks up, finally, at Gavin. Her heart continues an erratic racing rhythm. "How could you be so spiteful?" she says.

Gavin's eyes fill with tears. "That's not the way it was," he begins.

"You ruined two lives because of your spite." Magda stands up.

Everyone is quiet, unmoving. Then, Gavin collapses, his head falling forward into the sand.

The doctor comes, examines him, and finds nothing physically wrong with him.

Without Gavin and Colin, the group dissolves. Magda will never be forgiven.

During her last week, she goes to his door, and knocks several times a day, but he never answers, as if he recognizes her shadow. She slaps her hands against the closed door. Planes thunder overhead.

She hops buses, escapes into their familiarity. Day trips to Playa de Santiago, Manzanillo, El Colomo Cuyutlan, Pascuales. Night rides over a narrow ribbon of black through mountains and valleys. She finds herself in Guadalajara, Colima. The air thick with diesel fumes, moisture and dust. She could be anywhere.

The story she'll tell when she returns to Canada is that she flew down to Mexico to see her father, but he didn't recognize her.

Trademark: Flight, retreat, breakout, bolt. Outlaw, outcast, outrage.

People stream in and out of Gavin's room, carrying flowers, wines, fruit. They gag him with words, smiles, pats, so they won't have to listen to the screams of a man who would sell his house, abandon his friends and move to Mexico to escape himself, screams that echo those of a woman who would rather ride a bus all night than come home.

Sailing

That's my porch, on the hill. Right there. See the two planks? Look right above them and to the left. Yup. I can see everything that goes on at the dock from there. It's a small island, really, a harbour for lost souls — checked out of society, that's how I think of it. I can tell you about most everyone. Maybe things got too tough, too lonely, too painful, too something or other. Out here, you only deal with what you can. Cruise control.

Me, I'm from Washington State. I teach behavioural psychology at a small private college there. Weekends and summers I spend up here. I'm not trying to get away from anything. I like my job; I make good money; I have lots of friends. No. It's more like — floating. Here, I don't have to *do* anything. I don't have to *be* anything. Maybe

I'm a bit awkward around women. Am I being a bit awkward? You see, there hasn't been a woman in my life since my wife Celia. That was three years ago. At fifty-five, when you've been married to the same woman since you were twenty, it's difficult to learn how to date. Not that I'm trying, you understand. I like being on my own just fine. Go where I please. Do what I want. Not that I'm selfish, or anything. I just don't intend to spend my time looking for someone. It wouldn't do any good on an island this size. You pretty well know who's on and who's not. It's not like someone can swim over in the middle of the night.

So, you like sailing, huh? Good thing, 'cause there's not much else to do around here. A couple of general stores, a couple of restaurants, the pub at the landing. It's simple living. Most people have a boat. You get out on the waves. Go where the wind takes you. I think you'd like it here. Are you waiting for someone?

Gordie Fluxhall? You know him? Not bad for a man fifty-seven. Keeps in shape sailing that boat around. Going nowhere, though. He's got a cabin on the other side of the island, where you can't get at it, except by boat. Yeah, I've heard a few things about him. Don't know if they're all true, though.

For example, every month he puts an ad in the Campbell River, Nanaimo, Victoria and Vancouver newspapers. Must cost him a small fortune, at four dollars a line. In the ad, he says he wants a woman aged twenty-five to forty to go sailing around the world with him. Yeah. That's it. He's got posters, too. There's one in the laundromat, two doors down. Sometimes, I heard, he puts them in the women's washrooms. But I wouldn't know about that. Funny thing though, women answer the ads.

So far this month, there's been two. The first one was an eighteen-year-old Nanaimo girl. Came sailing in with her mother. She thought it was a job. You know. Cook and clean. A domestic, only on a waterhouse. So the mother goes down into the boat and has a look. And when she comes back up, she asks, "Where will she sleep?" And then she looks at Gordie's face, and she realizes this isn't a job, unless you're a hooker or something. Not that I'm implying that only hookers would answer the ads. I didn't mean that. But I can't imagine expecting a woman to sleep with me when she doesn't even know me. But Gordie, he's like that. He figures he's got it together: he doesn't have to work, and he's got something to offer — a free trip, a distraction from life for a few months. I don't know. Maybe he's thinking he'll fall in love one of these days. Doesn't seem likely to me.

After the teenager, he put an ad in the Portland paper. Told me he'd heard good things about Portland. I didn't know what he meant by that. Anyway, within a couple of days, he tells me a woman answered the ad and is arriving by plane in a week. He says to me, "Jim, could you go across and pick her up at the bus depot?"

I said yes, but she wasn't on the airport shuttle. So I took the first ferry back, and came down to the dock. And what do you think I see? This young woman, maybe thirty years old, looks Scandinavian. She's sitting on Gordie's boat, her bags around her.

Gordie waves me on. He's been drinking, I can tell, because his face is flushed. He's excited, too. Who wouldn't be with her sitting there? She's wearing cutoffs and a white T-shirt. Long blonde hair tied in a ponytail down her back. Green eyes and those high cheekbones. I don't usually notice physical details, you understand. But she was hard not to notice. So I joined them, because I was curious why she'd come up like that. I mean, Gordie could have been a pervert or a killer. She didn't know. So how could she trust him?

Gordie starts talking about the sailing trip. He takes out maps and starts pointing here and there. He's got routes marked in blue felt pen. He's got stopovers circled. He's got approximate dates of travel written in the margins. I wondered if Vivian (that was her name) would get to decide anything. Or would she just go for the ride? And then Gordie looked at her and said, "And I got a shotgun too. So we don't have to worry about nothing."

Vivian stared at me, alarmed. I smiled. I don't think Gordie's dangerous. I mean, he does do weird things. Like, for instance, before this sailing thing, he was putting in ads for women to come and live with him. And, believe it or not, a slew of them came. But he told me he had this rule, you see. They could only stay a month. "Too dangerous otherwise," he said. So I asked him, "For whom?" And he laughed, like he does when he doesn't want to answer. Anyway, he told the women the rule as soon as they arrived, and they must have agreed to it, 'cause all winter, one woman left on the last day of the month and the next one arrived on the first. I guess he slept alone that one night. Or maybe he spent it clearing all the evidence.

Just once, I remember, a woman stayed only three days. Gordie, alone for the month, scared everyone. Spent evenings shooting rounds into the air out at his place. Wasn't hurting anyone, but we could hear the shots. Eerie. You know? It kind of scares you, stuff like that. You can't really understand it. Or maybe you can, and that's what scares you. But I've never had a gun. I don't believe in violence.

So anyway, I reassured Vivian with my smile. She relaxed a bit, I could see that. And when Gordie suggested they go up to his house, she quickly invited me to come.

I didn't want to go there, but I said, "Let's have dinner at the pub."

So again, she looked relieved. Gordie shrugged and made some suggestive remark about time enough later. I felt embarrassed for him, because clearly this woman was not the type. But Gordie's not very observant. He's a handsome man, and he's used to getting his way. He exudes confidence and I guess women are attracted to that. You can like him or not, and he doesn't give a damn.

So all through dinner, Gordie is interjecting off-colour lines, touching her arm while he talks, winking. She kept looking at me after each of these. And she asked a lot about me, almost as if she was making sure *I* was okay. She should have been making sure Gordie was okay instead. Anyway, the evening eventually ended and the two of them got in the boat and went to his place. I walked up the hill and watched the boat until it rounded the point.

Next day, I came down as soon as I saw the boat coming in. She approached me immediately. "How well do you know him?" she asked.

"Not very," I said, which was true.

"He is positively the most horrible man I've ever met," she said. "Do you know he kept me up all night showing me all the food on board — enough to feed me for my entire life. I had to lock myself in the cabin." And then she asked me where she could get off the boat. She'd come this far, she said, she wanted to see the islands.

I told her there was a spot at Kelsey Bay. He'll pull in there. I saw it marked on his map. Vivian nodded thanks, then went into the store.

Gordie came over, after he'd fiddled with the boat awhile. "That is the worst woman I've ever met," he told me. "Do you know I spent the night trying to show her how I could provide for her — it's a long way around the world. I showed her all the supplies. You know. To prove I could take care of her. But she didn't care."

I hung around the dock for a bit, until Vivian came back and the two of them set off in the boat. Then I took a ferry and went over to Campbell River for the night. Change of pace. Stayed at the hotel there. Had a few laughs with the regulars. They all know me.

Then, the next day, when I got back, I heard Gordie'd been looking for me. He was alone, and he was carrying the shotgun. So I worried a bit that he was mad I'd told Vivian about Kelsey Bay. But Gordie's not that crazy.

The next time I saw Gordie was a few days later. He'd just put a new poster in the laundromat, and didn't wait for me to walk to the end of the dock. He touched his hat, and steered the boat out.

So you see, you might want to think about it. I mean, I'm only telling you because you asked. If it doesn't work out, I've got a spare room in my house. You're welcome to stay. And I don't expect you to do all the cooking and cleaning either. You're free to do as you like. There's a big yard out back, and the view's fantastic from the deck up there. You can just stare out, read a book, tell stories, whatever. I'm not a demanding kind of person. And like I said, I don't own a gun or anything.

Models

I. **Beauty Foils Rapist**

IT'S SUPPERTIME, A COLD JANUARY EVENING. THE DOORS ARE locked. A woman is feeding her cat when the window shatters and a man flies into the room, scatters shards across the floor — Evil Knievel without his motorcycle.

She is too astonished to move before he pulls the gun from his jacket pocket and tells her to strip.

And she does, slowly (the gun still pointed at her head), slowly (reluctance not seduction), while the cat flattens itself under the couch and all she can think of is that list her mother gave her, "*Twenty-five Ways A Single Woman Can Protect Herself*," and she wonders whether it was something she did or didn't do, and all the while she keeps stripping, slowly. Naturally, she thinks about sinking to her knees, clasping her hands and praying: Please, rapist god, don't hurt me, I won't tell anyone, I'll do what you want, I don't want to die. But she can smell the excitement of a hunt, his lips half-open, his eyes unblinking, her own scent — make a sudden movement and he'll be on her. She thinks this, while stripping. And the man's hand is dropping, until she's down to her panties and digging inside her brain for her mother's voice, for what must be somewhere within those women rules — the one, maybe, about stroking his ego, the stupid bastard.

She strokes the flat below her navel; her lips form: handsome, strong, want.

He pauses.

(Strange how in the beginning she was naked, then after the serpent and the apple (choose a metaphor), she's scrambling for fig leaves and clothes and words (which make excellent disguises). And how in this new guise, she is expected to disrobe, disclose, expose. And gradually, this stripping, this peeling off layers becomes an armour, a weapon, a Trojan horse. Can't he feel the knots in her hands? her lead heart? She strips and strips, shucks off veneer; her mind reshapes itself to shears — strips him of hair and strength and weapons. An eye for an eye — put him in a ring with King Kong, lock him in a cage with a grizzly, any of a million ways to show him that the last thing he deserves is an ego stroke, miserable coward.)

Her lips form: dinner, movies, flowers, champagne.

He pauses, gun lowered.

Romance, *love*.

He puts the gun aside and waits while she dresses, feeds the cat; waits through the drive to the restaurant, the dinner, wine, the bill please. Waits and waits while she goes to the bathroom and dials 9 1 1.

> (In the magazine article, the story ends here — *Beauty Foils Rapist* — bad guy caught; woman saved; happy ending.)

Later, when she retells the story to her friends, they laugh. Rapists don't come through windows at suppertime, they say. You must have known him, they say. Why did you strip? they ask. What did you have for dinner? Why aren't you dead?

> (Truth is that all around us women are stripping — on buses, in magazines, at newsstands, on billboards, in drug stores, on TV, in movies, in videos. They are so naked, we don't see them any more.)

And this woman, this *starlet,* as the article describes her (meaning cheap slut), this woman who duped her would-be rapist, did she go home triumphant? Fearless? Or did she buy bars for her windows, bolts for her doors? Did she move up to the twenty-sixth floor? Put an electrified fence around the balcony rail, barbed wire, an alarm system connected to a security post, motion detectors, night lights and a gun under her pillow?

(The trouble with real life is that some endings come, unexpected, and some go on forever.)

In the magazine, the woman with her cat and star dreams stares out from the margins — a promo photo — electric blue spandex bodysuit unzipped to the waist, eyes seducing the camera. You can almost hear skin tearing.

II. How To Behave

SHE IS ESTONIAN, HE GERMAN. THE FIRST TIME SHE SEES HIM, HE'S pointing a camera at her, so she can't see his eyes. He photographs her until her parents lead her away. She's fifteen. When she turns her head to look back at him, he's still hidden behind the lens.

On their wedding day, he gives her a book entitled *How A German Wife Should Behave*. This is during The War.

The book is a black rectangle and fits discreetly into her hand. The wife reads the book and follows the instructions. She's aproned and coiffed, her hands white, restrained by cotton gloves or flour. She practises ways to sit and smile, like the stylish black-and-white women etched on every page. She practises how to fold her hands, cross her legs, shape her lips to say "Yes." She buys a dictionary and thesaurus and memorizes the possibilities of the word

Behave: to handle, to exercise, to employ, to act, bear, carry, comport, serve, to follow, heed, mind, obey.

Sometimes, when no one is looking, she spreads the book open in her purse. The women roll off its pages, peel off gloves, clothes, shoes and husbands, and tumble into the satin lining, relieved, exhausted, like life-drawing models who have held a pose too long.

After The War, the husband takes her to Canada where they live in harmony — which is to say they don't divorce. She does not speak English, but when she asks if she can take lessons, the husband tells her she has no need for language. He will be her voice, and anyway, she has the book. What else does she need? He befriends German couples in which the women speak no English and behave like the book says. He points to the chapter "Learning to Laugh":

> The careful culture of the laugh should be attended to. The good wife must learn to sing a descending octave staccato on the syllable, Ha, ha, ha ... A word of warning: the inculcated laugh is apt to grow stereotyped, and few things are more irritating than to hear it over and over again, begin on the same note, run down the same scale, and consequently express no more mirth than the keys of a piano.

The wife frowns at this, and makes furtive attempts to practise, but the book doesn't explain about major keys and intervals, so her laugh comes out in a minor mode, and her husband tells her to stop that moaning.

The first few years, she reads and rereads the chapter in the book entitled "Your New Family," takes her temperature, times her period, visits doctors. When nothing happens, she re-reads the chapter, buys new lingerie, puts on soft music, lipstick and perfume. Finally, her husband whispers it's all right if she can't conceive. She doesn't contradict him, relieved, exhausted, although she knows she's not barren.

A good German wife should be healthy-minded and therefore not given unduly to introspection. She should not waste time on fruitless self-analysis, and should be content to leave herself unsolved.

Without children, they have much time. The husband fills the fridge with canisters of film, turns the rec room bathroom into a darkroom into which he disappears for hours. She fills the basement drawers with Easter paraphernalia — paints and brushes, tiny yellow bunnies, purple ribbons, etc. — the crafts of her Estonian background. In a hidden box in the attic, however, she keeps a carton of hollow eggs on which she paints the intricate lives of creatures who misbehave. If her husband could see these, he would mistake them for landscapes. He wouldn't notice that she has painted her own face and body on fence posts, roofs, leaves.

She is still a wife who knows how to behave as a German wife should behave, but her husband no longer appreciates this, because they now live in Canada, and he wants a wife who behaves like a Canadian wife should behave. Four months a year, he ships her off to visit her Estonian relatives. She goes happily, and tells everyone about her thoughtful German husband who remembers her Estonian heritage in Canada.

The husband sighs when she leaves. He doesn't know what he wants, or maybe he does. He wants to come home from work and find his dinner on the table, his carpets vacuumed, the house clean and silent; he wants his wife lounging in Saran Wrap, legs and lips open, inviting, her mind a blank reel on which his words imprint. (Secretly, though he'd never admit it to anyone, he also wishes he had a wife who could make up her own mind, be completely independent, who could make him suffer a little.)

The book says: *Can anything be nicer than a really nice girl?*

While his wife is gone, the husband hires women to come to his house so he can photograph them naked. The women do as he tells them (which is what good German wives do, too). They take off their clothes and lie in awkward positions while he prods and photographs them. The women know how to behave because they're being paid. Before his wife's return, the man stashes the women's photos and phone numbers in the basement, in the box where he keeps his lenses.

When the wife returns from her journeys, the house is always spotless, as if the husband has spent the entire time cleaning. She appreciates his tidiness; he appreciates the fact that she never asks what he did while she was away.

They go on like this, more or less, until one day, the man dies. In a box in the basement, she finds the women posed in her house, across her couch, on her pillow, legs splayed, mouths open, quite unlike the book said German wives should behave.

In the chapter, "Etiquette of Mourning," she finds a detailed discussion on appropriate garbs of grief: the texture and elegance of black deep-mourning dresses and gloves. Widows' weeds, she thinks, imagining wildflowers growing in her bed.

She takes a sheet of paper, folds it once and writes on the front, *How A Widow Should Behave When Her Bastard Husband Dies*. Inside, she writes, "Dance." When she opens her mouth, a perfect octave of descending notes spills out.

III. Widow Forced To Live With Corpse

Armenian village, Antoruk. Just past dawn, past dressing and pray-ing, a young woman lugs her husband out to the village courtyard and leans him against the wall, against other women's husbands, their stiff limbs thunking against one another. She kisses him good-bye, or maybe she feigns the brush of her lips against his cheek. Freed from the weight of her husband, she walks home at a quick-er pace, almost skipping. Ten years he has been dead, stuffed, injected, docile.

The Armenian widow belongs to the dead man's family. At night, his brothers, cousins, uncles slip into her bed to father new chil-dren (that's how they justify it). In ten years, she's had hundreds of visitations, and two children.

At dusk each evening, she carries her husband's stiff remains back into her home. Sometimes, she wonders what would happen if she simply dropped him into a ditch at the side of the path. Would he lie there forever, head packed with tree resin and sawdust, his heart perfectly preserved, and stare upwards in mock prayer?

(You wonder how religious this embalming is, and whether aromatic substances, disinfecting fluids and preservative powders amply prepare a man for his life after death, and his widow for a life after him.)

Across the world, here too, embalmed men everywhere. Lodged into golf carts, strip bars, yacht decks, leather airplane seats, mahogany office chairs; in front of TVs, hockey games, demolition derbies, software fairs. Some men embalm themselves. The trick is to find the countless ways to die daily and still come home at night.

In the daytime, the women prop these men in front of screens, wait for the blue reflection in their husbands' eyes, kiss their cheeks, pat their arms, and off they go, freed for another day to do whatever they can, given their social and financial positions. They work, shop, raise children, remodel homes, build roads, write books, sing, dance and join daytime circuses. And these men's brothers, cousins, uncles, friends, too, are concerned about the poor wives left alone, their embalmed husbands propped downtown. They sneak the women into their beds and make surrogate love. Of course, they talk about guilt, but only while undoing a shirt or the silver buckle of a black sandal. These women's children bear their husbands' names and, without DNA testing, who's to know?

The Armenian woman accepts protection — she has no choice.

She can't exactly buy herself back: get a job and move into a three-bedroom condo with five appliances; check out internet chat sites for singles; join Widows Anonymous and go on Caribbean cruises and bus tours to China. She can't even divorce the dead (too shameful). Easier to keep the marriage going; easier to keep the corpse beside her, heart quivering.

Tabloids

Pick up the remote, turn on the TV and feast on a harlequin of squalor. It's six o'clock. Bad news on every channel: rapes and murders, extortions and thefts, stabbings and nabbings, prostitutions, executions. Flick fast enough and the violence blurs into rubbish and cockroaches and stripbars and bruises and beer and bloodstains. On TV, grime and crime go together like horse and carriage. And you wonder, who are these people? Groveling and desperate. Not starched and tidy like white-collar criminals, who aren't called this, and whose offenses are nonthreatening and more like educated pranks. (You can admire the Robin-Hoodness, the clean bookwork, the brains.) They don't rob and murder, they embezzle and manslaughter, their indiscretions relegated to later in the newscast, like headliners at a concert.

But right now, the opening acts unscramble: PARENTS PARTY WHILE CHILDREN PERISH. You frown and follow the tabloid camera down narrow corridors and stairs; break down a door and freeze the startled faces. Who are these people? Not ones you recognize. Mid-dance, bottles in hand. Pupils torpid, eyelids sagging. Zoom in, see the syringe still clinging to an arm? See children and cockroaches scurrying and vying for dog food on the floor?

No. This wouldn't be you or anyone you know, because most of you don't have children and those who do, have polite, clean ones. And this is because you are all educated, and know about birth control (though you call it family planning) and prefer thinking to drinking or, at the very least, thinking while drinking (moderately, of course — the drinking, that is). And you might have one friend who hasn't always been moderate, but certainly he has been since you've known him, and now he goes to AA meetings and stays home a lot more, although the house is empty — his wife and children gone long ago — and he drinks pop when he visits and he talks about calling his children and maybe having them come and live with him, but he hasn't done it as long as you've known him and that's been years.

And you wonder if he's watching the newscast and if it conjures memories. But you'd never ask him because you don't want to know, because you don't want to be uncomfortable when you watch these newscasts together, because you want to be able to shake your head and ask, "Who are these people?" and have your friends nod and shake their heads, and turn off the TV and put on classical music and talk about important things.

And suddenly, a commercial explodes onto the screen. Graphic simulation/manipulation. Sound: strains of "We Are Family," sampled and buried in a myriad of effects. Multi-cultural-coloured faces super-imposed on each other, uniting. And you marvel how they share one set of eyes — the symbolism not lost to you — although you know intellectually that this is simplistic and romantic, given that within your own family it's hard to find two people who see eye-to-eye, so to speak. In fact, you think, some of your nastiest memories are of times when your family united.

Take, for example, that long weekend you agreed to meet at Silverstar Mountain for a family ski extravaganza. Picture it: a six-bedroom chalet — a couple in each, and the four children on cots. It's the first time you invited Dylan to meet your family, thinking all that cold air and thick snow would surely keep things cool. But of course, it doesn't, and before you know it, the room is sizzling and each of you retreats to your battle stations — father and daughters on one side, mother on the other, and brothers and Dylan acting as observers. It's slash and burn for a while, then sud-denly you feel the current shift, fickle, searching a new commo-tion. It spirals and twists around the room until *you* are its epicen-tre: *you* are leading a questionable life and Dylan here (desperately trying to blend into the wallpaper) is concrete evidence of your instability. You tell them to leave Dylan out of it. And then some-one says, "Why did you bring him if you want him left out of it?" So you shout above the chaos, "Let's just take a little inventory on marriages in this family. Or maybe we should do divorces?" At which point, you're told to shut up and leave if you don't like it. Which you do, taking a bewildered Dylan with you out into the snow for a four-hour walk-and-coffee-drinking-in-the-café because you don't want to go back in and get your skis, or better still, your suitcase and the keys to your car. And you wonder why it always starts with this-time-I'll-be-tolerant but, by the end of the weekend, degenerates into I-could-just-kill-them.

But you don't mean this, of course, not really, not like the newscast: TEENS BRUTALLY MURDER MOTHER AND FATHER. Not like the two sobbing boys for whom you feel tear jerks, because they couldn't possibly have killed their parents without good cause. And the anchors are only too happy to oblige and outline in graphic, sordid detail exactly what this good cause is. And you nod your head and your friends nod too, even though you know intellectually that this is simplistic and that human beings have been murdering each other forever, and not always with good cause. And while you ponder this, the camera freezes the solemn face of the teenage murderer against blue background: *Close shot: greyish skin, pockmarks on cheeks and chin, eyelids purple and swollen.* Then fade out. And this symbolism isn't lost to you either. You can almost see the Bible open to the right page, and hear the words "An eye for an eye," or is it "Let he who etc. cast the first stone"? But before you can decide which one it is, the screen erupts into a rap song. Three teenage girls kick and twirl and cartwheel while their clothing mutates in a rapid reel of colours. Cut-out dolls. Mix-and-match. The sequence ends with the department store logo superimposed on the three teens who collapse in a heap of hugs in the corner of the screen. You can almost taste the "Material" mouths of these Madonnas. Kiss, kiss. Hug, hug. You can almost hear the strains of "We Are Family."

And you think how appropriately simplistic and romantic to omit the rivalries and frictions, the strifes and furious competitions/suspicions/oppositions. Unlike the story on the screen. TEENAGE GIRL UNDERGOES HAIRLIFTING EXPERIENCE. A fifteen-year-old, having fought with a girlfriend over a sweater or a boyfriend, solicits the help of two girlfriends (also fifteen) and the three of them ambush the enemy after school, kidnap her, hold her at knife point, then cut off her long blonde hair. Whew! Well. Who are these people? you think. You can't imagine any of your women friends, knife in hand, threatening anyone.

Actually, there is someone, but she's certainly not your friend. She's more like family. All right, she *is* family, or was family until that nightmare birthday party. Sally is your mother's brother's daughter, which makes her your cousin whether you like it or not. As long as you've known her, she has performed a diatribe on the inequalities between siblings. More specifically, she detests her younger brother, Jim, a musician who, in her opinion, "is a talentless bum who does nothing but sleep and booze and fuck." On her father's sixtieth birthday, while you're all in the living room playing charades, Sally starts a minor war with Jim. When you go to the kitchen for ice, you find Sally jabbing a coat hanger at Jim, inches from his throat. In her other hand is the pair of scissors she was using to make paper doilies for the dessert plates. You scream, which brings everyone running, and for the next few minutes you're all trying to negotiate the implements out of Sally's hands. Not only are you all unsuccessful, but in one of her jabs, Sally grabs Jim's glasses, throws them on the floor and stamps on them. (Try sampling a bit of this music.) Her father and yours eventually subdue her, and the casualties remain inanimate:

a ripped shirt, a jacket with a severed sleeve and a pair of broken glasses. Her husband takes her home (later you hear she's in therapy) and that's the end of Sally. You don't speak about her and neither does anyone else in the family. So, she doesn't really count, does she?

And the rest of you are all mature enough to resume your lives and not loiter over personality clashes that could lead to physical injury like the family on TV: MOTHER AND FATHER MURDER DAUGHTER-IN-LAW AND STUFF HER IN A CAR TRUNK. Who are these people? And you think, whew, thank goodness your cousin Sally is in therapy. Or is it a support group?

Original sin is hard to find these days. Private pain even harder. And please, no individual acts. Keep it simple. Keep it in a group. Kiss, kiss. Hug, hug. There, there. Pack angst. Have no friends? Pick a vice and join the appropriate support group. Then you can all have your fifteen minutes of fame: get on a stage, beat your breast (mea culpa) while secretly searching for admiring glances. See how bad I am? And how good too, to publicly denounce myself. Gives you ammunition to admonish others. Mass mortification. Gang guilt. A mutual-admiration validation society: verbal masturbation — S&M style.

And suddenly there it is, an advertisement for a *weekend workshop* (coming to a hotel near *you*). GET IN TOUCH WITH YOUR INNER CHILD. Well, you think, are we talking schizophrenia here or what? Then you shrug and look around, guilty, hoping no one heard you. You know what happened last June at the garden party, when you made a similar comment and Aunt Joan glared at you through clenched teeth and stiffly informed you that "schizophrenia is a disease and incurable, though controllable." And you realized suddenly that she had it and that no one had ever told you, and you wondered who was she otherwise. But you didn't ask her because you were afraid she'd knife you or hack you with an axe or whatever, like schizophrenics do on TV. Which they're not doing now, because a very sensitive, NewAge man is earnestly telling the camera that he can *help you find your inner child.* Well, you've seen plenty of people's inner children and, quite frankly, some of them should have stayed lost. You recall, in fact, when your Uncle Henry, at the age of fifty-two, not only found his inner child, he decided to give it a mate. There was that embarrassing family dinner when he brought the teenager with the single-syllable vocabulary. Kiss, kiss. Hug, hug. Fortunately, six months later, he buried his inner child and begged Aunt Joan to take him back (which she did), and now nobody mentions it.

Then, after the sports clips, the weather clowns, the ads for untold-stories-of-the-week, the anchor says, "Coming up, a human-interest story." And you think, great, what were the last forty-five minutes? At whom were those stories aimed? Human interest? Read: sappy, happy stories. The kind that prompt involuntary tears. FIREMAN RESCUES CAT FROM OAK TREE, or AMNESIA VICTIM REUNITED WITH FAMILY. And you're still wondering, who are these people? Because you've never seen a cat skeleton in a tree, or a fireman walking around your neighbourhood. And you've never met anyone with amnesia, unless you count your best friend, Barbara, who used to smoke hashish a lot and forget things. But the last thing she needed was a reunion with the family.

And finally, it's LOTTO 6/49. Now this, you think, is a human-interest story. You fish the lottery ticket out of your wallet. Look at the numbers: 30 and 06 — the day and month of your first marriage;

12, 16 and 27 — the days your divorces became final; and 38 — your age. You're not superstitious; you only choose the same numbers every week because you know the odds get better. Never mind that you'd have to play several million weeks. People do win, you say, when your friends' eyebrows arch. You've seen them right there on TV. Kiss, kiss. Hug, hug. And not only that, winners are apple-pie and violin-soaring happy; they never quit their jobs or their mates. They share their wealth with family and friends, and never argue. No grime and crime on Lotto 6/49. Kiss, kiss. Hug, hug. You want to win. But a part of you knows the probability is slim that you could ever be one of these people on TV.

Couplets

Amy sits at one of the sixty bars along the strip, thinking about how things go together: *rum and Coke, love and marriage, rock and roll, separation and divorce*. She tries to find a complement for *custody*. But all she can think of is *battle*.

It's late February, that time of year when the ice begins to break, snow melts, and people swarm in from all directions, with winter stories and cabin fevers. Breakup time. The Sourdough Rendezvous. The town's crammed and frolicking.

She took the solo gig in Whitehorse — a month in a piano bar — because of her band's spontaneous combustion a week ago. She packed her singed ego, electric piano, satin camisoles, slipdresses, platform shoes, and the bitter taste of friends turned enemies (like chewing kumquats in reverse), and rode the train home. Calgary to Vancouver. Third roomette on the right, which turned out to be the wrong side of the train for viewing anything except the claustrophobic face of a white mountain. Spindly trees leaned forward, heavy with snow. Now and then, a wild branch slapped the window. On the other side, if she cared to go and look, she'd see a void, and herself as the implausible shore of a canyon that plunged deeper than despair.

Amy took the gig in Whitehorse because it was the only one available on such short notice, and because she's rehearsing her new solo act. Maybe, if she can get steady work in town, Jason will let her have Blair longer than a Sunday.

Around the piano, men slouch on high stools, their backs curved forward, like shields. They stare straight ahead, or down the chasms into their drinks. Loneliness, Amy thinks, is about abandonment. Are there sons or daughters somewhere, longing for these men? Or are these men yearning for their own fathers or mothers, husbands and wives, lovers and friends? She stirs her drink and sighs. She has not abandoned her son, she thinks. And she is not a *flake*, as her ex-husband calls her. She's a *musician,* and that spells *flexible, go-where-the-work-is*. It doesn't mean she's a bad mother. Tell that to her ex-husband and his fucking fancy lawyer.

Horse and carriage. Life and death. Mother and son.

She takes her caesar backstage, and calls Blair.

"Daddy's going to take me to Disneyland!" His five-year-old voice wavers with excitement.

"That's lovely, sweetheart." Amy chokes back the lump swelling in her throat. He's bribing the child, she thinks, but there's nothing she can do.

"And I'm going to see Mickey Mouse and Minnie, and I'm going to ride all the rides, and everything!"

"You're going to have a wonderful time, darling." She blows her nose. "I miss you, sweetie. Do you miss me a little bit?"

"Yes." He pauses, and she's not sure what's in the space.

She tries to imagine the child's point of view. Blair has not lived with her since Jason found out about her affair with the drummer. Eight months ago. She's been on the road ever since.

"Mommy, why don't you come to Disneyland with us?" he says, his voice anxious to please her.

"Darling, if I could, I would," she says. "Mommy's far far away right now."

"Daddy says Disneyland is far away, but we're going to go in a jet. Bruuum, bruuum, and we're there!"

IN THE DAYTIME, SHE BUNDLES UP AND WALKS DOWN MAIN street, engulfed in a mushroom cloud of testosterone. All morning, there are contests that test male strength — like flour-sack packing — and survival skills, such as animal-skinning under frigid conditions. They ought to test motherhood, Amy thinks, walking past them to the river. *The Yukon*, the brochure said, *flows for 2897 km, and empties into the Bering Sea.* A continuous cycle, like her own blood traveling the map of her body day in, day out. She walks along the shoreline, imagining water flowing beneath the wide expanse of snow-covered ice. Like secrets. Or love. A frigid wind whips her. Her nostrils bristle with frost. Now and then, the ice cracks in gunshot sounds that startle her.

Along the banks, mushers prepare their dog teams. *Snow and ice.*

Dogs and sleds. Amy stops often, stares at the huskies' mismatched, patchwork eyes. Green, violet, brown, white, blue, like marble explosions.

At first, she doesn't notice the boy among the huskies. Grey parka, hood up and cinched under his chin, his small white face framed by animal fur, he carefully brushes the dogs' thick coats. Now and then, one turns and licks his hand, his face. He's about six or seven. Alone.

"Hi," she says.

He does not look up.

She smiles. "Those your dogs?"

The boy continues his grooming.

She squats next to him, her chest billowing with yearning. Blair can never concentrate on anything for very long, his small body constantly in motion. This boy is still and serious. "Do you go to school?" she asks.

He stares at her, silent.

"What do you want?" A man's voice, behind her.

Amy turns. "Oh. You must be his father," she says. The man is six-foot-four or -five, with a bushy red beard and pale green eyes. He's carrying a harness.

"What do you want?" he says again.

She stands up. "I was just … curious," she says. "I saw your boy and … I have a boy …" She stops, because the man, like his son, is unmoving against the background of snow, the albescent river of ice. "You see, I don't have my boy with me," she says quickly, "and your son reminded me …" She bites her lip.

The man turns his back and begins to harness the dogs. The boy scrambles up to help him.

Amy watches for a moment. "How come he's not at school?" she asks.

"My son is my business," the man says, his face impassive. Abruptly, he steps forward, until his large body is within a foot of Amy, clearly violating her space.

She steps back, and he forward again, until she understands and leaves.

"THAT'S THE WOLFMAN'S SON," THE BARTENDER TELLS HER later. "Deaf. Dad claims he's home-schooling him."

"Does he have a mother?"

"Somewhere." The bartender shrugs. "The wolfman must have moved here maybe five years ago. Bought a gold mine in the woods somewhere. Least, that's how I heard it. He was on his own, with the baby. He doesn't hang out, and he doesn't like people."

"I noticed," Amy says.

"Rumour has it he's got a wolf."

"A wolf?" She frowns, recalling a TV documentary about a man who captured a wolf cub and raised it as a pet.

"That's what they say. Maybe it's to guard the gold. Or maybe, he's the wolf." He laughs. "Bad news," he says, and Amy hears *intriguing*, hears *aphrodisiac*; hears *this is the most fabulous, difficult man on the face of the Earth.*

EACH DAY NOW, AMY GOES TO THE RIVER. SHE BRINGS THE BOY small gifts — toy trucks, a hockey stick, a book — which he accepts shyly. Tries them out when he thinks his father is not watching. The wolfman turns his head away, but Amy recognizes the bittersweet acknowledgement that the boy has needs he can't fulfill.

Eight months ago, when Jason uncovered her affair, he gave her an ultimatum — quit work or quit the marriage. She picked the latter, given that she had awakened from a six-year stupor, and found herself muzzled and yoked, unlike the woman she used to be.

AT NIGHT, SHE SITS AT THE PIANO, PLAYING TUNES OUT OF HER cheatbook — a binder that contains no music, only lyrics and chord patterns. Like the cheatbook, the piano, too, is a skeleton: a hollow, wooden, grand-piano body, the front of which is fitted with an electric keyboard. A heart transplant, only this time the heart's been taken out and replaced with wires, electronics. A nonsensical simulation that people don't notice. They trust their eyes, and lean their elbows on the black lacquered tongue.

An oversized brandy snifter languishes on the shiny top. At ten o'clock, people are still arriving; some are two drinks in. Soon, men will request songs — memory-jolts — and drop in loonies, toonies, fivers, as gratitude.

All week, just past 10 p.m. (after the boy's asleep?), the wolf-man appears at the piano bar. He drinks quietly and slowly, staring into his glass. Now and then, from the inside pocket of his jacket, he takes a black velvet pouch, unties it, and shakes it gently into his palm. Nuggets fall out, all sizes and shapes. He chooses one, and puts it in her snifter.

She's been gathering them, these gold contours. The wolfman always leaves in the middle of her last set. She's waiting for him to ask her out, but he never does.

At the end of her second week, on her Sunday off, she heads into the woods. For a walk, she tells herself, fresh air, exercise. But her heart flutters. She asked the staff where the wolfman lives, and they pointed to this direction, although none of them have been here. She wonders if they've invented the stories, if he's simply an eccentric hermit with a small boy. The trail meanders to the left, to the right; she's never quite sure in what direction. She shivers, thinking *it was much safer being in that other life*.

Then, up ahead, a large animal. Yellow-grey coat patched in black and white. A German shepherd, perhaps. Or a wolf. She pauses, breath held, watches the bared teeth, the round intense pupils. The animal strides toward her, and she doesn't know whether to run or not.

"Serge!"

The wolf stops, cocks its head to the left. The wolfman calmly strolls toward them, rifle slung over his shoulder. He slaps his thigh, and the animal obeys, but its eyes remain focused on Amy. When he's within arm's reach, the man collars the wolf.

Amy exhales; her knees buckle.

"Where are you going?" the wolfman asks.

She bites her lip. Isn't it perfectly obvious that she was coming to find him? She shakes her head. "I'm … I was out for a walk."

They stare at each other, both still. "You shouldn't be walking in the woods alone," he says, finally. "It's dangerous. This isn't a city, you know."

"Is that a wolf?" Amy asks, stepping forward.

He moves back, away from her, in tandem to her movement. "Respect the animal's space," he says, and she stops. "Always leave it room to escape. Then it will trust you."

She waits, uncertain, while he slowly closes in, along with the wild creature whose pungent scent overwhelms her. She could turn and run, she thinks. When they are face to face, the man drops the leash, and the wolf pads toward her. She stands perfectly still while it explores her slowly, its nose brushing against her, its breath hot, its fur rough against her hands. She stands perfectly still, frightened, not frightened, hyperconscious of the animal, the danger, the man who arouses her with his proximity, with his wilful distance.

In her mind, a tape loop: *Few if any reports exist of unprovoked wolf attacks on humans.*

She turns and flees down the path.

That night, when she opens the motel door, he is framed against the night sky. She opens herself to his slow exploring, her hands echoing his. Falls asleep in his arms, and in the morning finds him gone.

IN THE TV DOCUMENTARY, THE WOLF DIDN'T KNOW IT WAS A wolf; it had been raised with a German shepherd pup, in captivity. It yelped and barked and lay in front of the TV, at the foot of its master. Now and then, however, something would trigger its wolf nature and render it dangerous. On a camping trip, after a swim in the lake, when the German shepherd came out of the water, the wolf attacked it, forcing it back into the lake until it almost drowned. Another time, when it chanced upon cattle, the wolf rolled in dung to mask its scent, then circled the herd, searching for the most vulnerable animal.

EACH DAY NOW, WHILE THE WOLFMAN IS AT THE MINE, AMY plays with the boy and teaches him words. "Wolf," she says, pointing to the animal. "Wolf." They're outside, and a puff of steam escapes with each *w*. The boy laughs, delighted, blowing small breaths, his lips formed into an *o*.

Even when the wolfman returns, the boy sits beside Amy, and fingers her clothes and objects around them. She mouths the names of what he touches; takes his other hand and holds it against her lips. Then moves his fingers against his mouth, while he shapes silent words.

Sometimes, she sees the wolfman watch her with the boy. He is so unlike the men she knows, who are constantly yapping, demanding her attention, her sympathy, her admiration. The wolf-man speaks with his eyes, with small, powerful gestures. Yet each night, when they're in her motel room, and the boy is sleeping in the cabin, Amy begs him to tell her something personal.

ON THEIR LAST NIGHT TOGETHER, HE FINALLY SAYS, "WHEN Sylvia — that's my wife — and me split up, I took the baby and ran. We've never looked back."

She draws in her breath. "What do you mean, ran?"

"You know. She would have taken the boy."

Amy imagines herself frantic, searching for Blair. She'd never stop looking. She wants to phone Jason, make sure Blair's all right, make sure he's there. She almost gets up, then remembers they're in California. What if Jason was lying? What if at this very moment, her ex-husband is making himself invisible? What if she never sees Blair again? She knows it's absurd. She's no threat, and Jason's not that type of person. But her stomach lurches.

"What did she do? Your wife, I mean?" she asks.

He shrugs. "The boy's better off here."

"But doesn't he miss his mother?"

"He doesn't remember her," the wolfman says. "He was just a baby when we left."

How long is Blair going to be in California? she wonders. She looks at her watch, although it's too dark to see. Could he forget her in two weeks? A month? How long would it take? Her heart flip-flops.

The wolfman is quiet beside her. She should say something, acknowledge this secret, this trust. But all she can think about is Blair. She'll get a different job, maybe go back to school, get a degree so she can have a bigger apartment and stay home nights and stop traveling.

Husband and wife, she thinks. Plate tectonics.

"Aren't you afraid they'll find you?" she says, finally.

"We're a long way from home."

She doesn't say goodbye. Before her flight, when the wolfman and the boy are at the riverbank, she goes to the cabin, and leaves them each a parting gift: for the boy, a Mickey Mouse watch; for the wolfman, a brandy snifter, and the gold nuggets he gave her.

WHEN SHE OPENS THE DOOR TO HER APARTMENT IN Vancouver, she sees it as Jason must see it: unwashed dishes in the sink, dustballs coiling against the heaters, a mattress on the floor, two-by-fours and bricks for furniture. *Not fit for a child.* She sets her suitcase on a stolen hotel rack in the bedroom, and phones Jason.

"I'm having a birthday party," she tells him. "I want you and Blair here."

"Next Saturday?" Pages flip. "No," he says. "We're definitely booked. Sorry."

"Can't you let me have Blair for a little while?" she asks. "A couple of hours."

"Who's going to be there, Amy?" he says in his fatherly voice.

"Friends," she says. "It's my birthday, for God's sake!"

"Friends. Your *musician* friends?" he says, his voice sarcastic. "I don't want Blair around your flaky friends. I don't want him around alcohol, and I don't want him around drugs."

"It's not like that," she says, but already she's thinking *he's right*. She presses her fingers into her temples, wondering *why didn't I think of that?* Instead of mothering instincts, she feels a huge, gaping hole in her heart. "Lunch, then," she says. "Just me and him."

On Saturday, she watches Blair get out of the car, more little man than boy. He's wearing brown corduroy trousers and a checked tan-and-white shirt tucked in, the collar buttons done up. He runs up the steps and hugs her, Mickey Mouse between them.

After lunch, she gives him the miniature wolf she bought in Whitehorse.

He touches the wolf, uncertain. "Is it from *Little Red Riding Hood*?" he asks. "The bad wolf?"

"No, darling," she says. "It's a good wolf." She takes it out of the box. "Look at its beautiful eyes," she says.

"Wolves are scary, Mommy." He slaps the wolf. "Bad wolf!" he says. "You ate the little pigs. Bad!" and he slaps it again.

Amy sighs. "We'll just leave the wolf here, in the box, where it can't hurt anyone."

Blair picks up his Mickey Mouse and squeezes it against his chest.

AMY DRINKS HALF A BOTTLE OF WINE BEFORE THE GUESTS arrive. Mid-party, Jason turns up, unexpected. He hovers near the door, a smug look on his face. A spy, Amy thinks. She's wearing a lacy black slip, no bra; she laughs and dances in the centre of the room, aware that Jason is watching her, judging her.

Just past midnight, the buzzer sounds. When she opens the door, the wolf stares back at her, its eyes wary, disquieting. It's leashed. She stumbles back, to give it space. The wolfman pushes past her into the room, and everyone stops talking and "Ahhs" and "Oohs" over the wolf.

Amy follows, pulling at the wolfman's sleeve. "What are you doing here?" she whispers. "Where's the boy?"

"As if you care," he says. He reaches into his jacket pocket and pulls out the Mickey Mouse watch. "You didn't even say goodbye." He throws the watch against her chest.

The wolf snarls.

"Shut up," the wolfman says.

Amy scoops up the watch. "I didn't want to upset him —."

"Upset him?" he bellows, and shoves her back in two quick motions.

The wolf snarls again, bares its teeth, barks.

"Shut up," the wolfman says, pulling the leash tight.

But the wolf spooks and turns on him. It sinks its teeth into the wolfman's arm. Amy screams. The wolf shakes its head, tearing flesh.

The wolfman keeps repeating the animal's name, trying to calm it, and Amy herds everyone into the hall, crying and half-hysterical, terrified, thinking *the wolf must have misunderstood, it was trying to protect me,* thinking *its loyalties were tested.*

Finally, the animal lets go. It scuttles into a corner and licks itself.

"Your arm —" Amy begins, but the wolfman silences her with a look. He strokes the wolf, picks up the leash, and they stalk out, past the huddle of shocked people in the hall.

She stands in the middle of the room, thinking *everything and everyone is slipping away.*

"Who's the Neanderthal?" Jason says at her elbow. His face is puckered, as if he's just bitten into a lime. "Really, Amy," he says. "You really should see a therapist." He turns toward the door.

She breathes in, and suddenly scents overwhelm her. She wants to flee down the steps, take a taxi to the airport, find the wolfman, apologize; she wants to stay, get a job, be responsible, find Blair, apologize.

She follows Jason to the door, head reeling with her friends' laughter, distant and obnoxious.

"Jason," she pleads, and he turns.

In the TV documentary, when the wolf became too dangerous, the man released it into the wild. But the wolf had never been free, and was frightened. It tried to get back into the Wrangler. The man dug a drinking hole and filled it with water, hung a carcass of meat from a tree, then when he could see the wolf was despondent, took off his coat and left it on the ground, for comfort. Weeks later, when he returned to check on the animal, he found the wolf wandering at the side of the highway, trailing the coat in its mouth.

Measures

After dinner, while Brian restrings and tunes his guitar, Eve and Lydia clear the table and stack the plates in the dishwasher. Billy and Ned, five and three, sit on the floor, plates between their thighs, having food races. Eve tries not to slip.

"You needn't do this," Lydia tells her. "Go in and sing with him. I know you're dying to." Eve hasn't played with her brother, Brian, in fifteen years, but she knows it won't take long for it all to come back. He's working lounges now and tonight, Eve's going to sit in with him at Howlin' Joe's.

"Thanks." Before she goes into the living room, Eve gives Lydia a quick hug. This is not because she particularly likes Lydia, but to reward her for being sensitive for a change.

Eve drove up from Vancouver to visit them because a couple of months ago, Brian started to write her the familiar letters. Not letters, exactly. Dictionary definitions of specific words. It was how, in their teens, they used to summon each other when something was wrong. A private communication their parents wouldn't understand. For example, the first one he sent was

The Blues. *The Royal Horse Guards; the Conservatives; form of Negro and modern music expressing gaiety and sadness at the same time.*

Well, already Eve's seen this in action. The gaiety spills out of a rum bottle and the sadness out of the spill. Brian and Lydia are entrenched in routine. Brian gets up at noon and takes over babysitting the children. Lydia sits at the kitchen table, Brian's guitar in her arms. She pours her first drink before 2 p.m. She's not an obnoxious drunk, not the kind you easily identify. Lydia turns inward; her face darkens; her eyes trance to some other time and place. Now and then, she strums a string or two. The sound reverberates. "Come have a drink with me, honey-babe," she periodically calls out to Brian. He ignores her, but Eve can read the resignation in the curve of his shoulders. When she looks at him, questioning, he looks away.

Brian is leading a pathetic life, Eve thinks. The kind that belongs inside a folder at Social Services.

"Let's see what you got," she says to Brian now, flipping through his book for songs she knows. They rehearse beginnings and endings; settle keys and breaks. Eve feels a familiar comfort —

like coming home after a long trip and sleeping in her own bed. She has missed singing. A pure expression. To let her voice wrap itself around notes and words. The dynamics of tone — emotions unfettered in sound.

"How's good old Steven?" Brian asks. "Or should I say, young?"

"He's fine," Eve says, her voice defensive even to herself. Steven is twenty-six; she's thirty-seven. He might be fine, but according to him, she's not. Steven is constantly reminding her that she is not measuring up to his standards in just about everything. Intellectually, she understands they are at that point in the relationship when the fairydust begins to thin out and there is the sudden crystalline recognition of the other person as separate and distinct from oneself — an autonomous, thinking, feeling being whose opinions are not always agreeable. They are seesawing, she thinks. It used to be that Steven was trying to be older, to follow her examples. Now, he's so self-assured, he expects her to follow his.

"Why didn't he come up with you?" Brian asks.

"Too busy," Eve says vaguely. She doesn't want to think about Steven right now.

Brian's songlist is pages long — a repertoire of seven hundred and ninety-four songs. She recognizes many, but can't remember all the lyrics or the tunes. She asks him to play a few bars of this or that to remind her. While they are doing this, the children come, naked, into the room. There are chocolate milk rings stained over other stains around their mouths, wet toast bits in their hair and hands. It is like a TV image on *Cops*, when the camera pans inside run-down tenements filled with filthy children and filthy lives. Eve looks at Brian, her wonderful older brother who everyone thought would go so far in life. To be reduced to this. The children begin to chase each other around the coffee table, squealing like piglets. Eve tries to ignore them as they run faster, delirious, almost hysterical with excitement, their arms flailing into her legs, knocking Brian's pick out of his hand.

"Oh for God's sake," she says. "Can't Lydia take care of them? It's not like she's working or anything. Look at them. They're like savages!"

And, as if to emphasize her point, Billy grabs his brother from behind and Ned pees an arc around the coffee table and on Eve's shoes.

Brian erupts in laughter. Lydia comes from the kitchen to see what's funny. She joins in the laughter and the children, who at first were very still because of Eve's reaction, now encouraged by their parents, begin to spin wildly around. Like dancing monkeys, Eve thinks. Complete madness. How could her brother Brian sink into this squalor? It is only when Billy begins to pee into the air that Brian suddenly sobers up and says, "Enough. You go upstairs into the bathroom and do that."

LATER, AFTER BRIAN HAS GONE TO HOWLIN' JOE'S, EVE AND Lydia are in the bathroom, painting their nails, drying their hair. The children are asleep, and a sitter is coming soon.

"I'm really looking forward to this," Eve tells Lydia. "I miss singing so much." She hates to admit this, even to herself, as if she were exposing a vulnerability.

She stopped playing in bands when she turned thirty, because she didn't feel connected any more — people looked younger, sillier; she couldn't talk to them. For the next five years, she did solo gigs in the lounges of smart hotels downtown. But here too, she didn't feel connected — the crowd too old, too cynical; she couldn't talk to these people either. Music drew them together, but only in parallel lines that would never intersect.

"It must be hard," Lydia says, "to be living on your own. You and Wayne must have been together ... what? Eight? Nine years?"

"Ten," Eve says. "I didn't say I missed Wayne."

Lydia bends over and leisurely applies a second coat of red nail polish to her right toe. Eve admires the flat shiny surface of the nail, not at all like her own ridged one.

"You and Steven planning to move in?" Lydia asks when she straightens up.

"No."

"How long's it been? One? Two years?"

"Are we keeping count?" Eve says, then adds, "About two." She bends down and applies the second coat to her own toenails. "He's been asking," she says, after a moment, because she doesn't want Lydia to get the wrong idea. Steven's been hinting. Often, he takes her on "architectural tours," as he calls them. House-hunting. Steven is an architect, constantly redesigning. "... I'd take out this wall; put in a pony wall here — glass bricks, of course, to let in more light; get rid of those windows and put in a skylight — more privacy ..." Steven can look at an old house and see a modern palace. All it takes is a little demolition and rebuilding. Like sculptors who chip away what's unnecessary. Like the time he bought her a black slipdress and teeny crocheted cardigan to replace her favourite blue suit that was "too straight and makes you look older." Or when his friends were coming to dinner and Steven put all her treasures in a box because "they're junk and belong in flea markets."

She sighs. She has not come to visit her brother to discuss her personal life with his wife.

"Things okay with you and Brian?" she asks.

Lydia shrugs. "Comes and goes. Good and bad periods. But isn't that what life is all about?"

It can't be easy living in this small dump, Eve thinks, trying to be sympathetic, although she believes nothing happens on its own; good and bad are made. Brian and Lydia moved here eight years ago, right after Lydia was asked to resign from St. Mary's School for Girls, amid rumours of inappropriate behaviour. More specifically, a student's mother accused her of having a lesbian relationship with her daughter. Lydia denied it, then had a nervous breakdown. They came to Onion River because a friend of Lydia's had grown up there and had inherited a house she was willing to sell cheap. Eve tried to dissuade Brian. How could he abandon a promising career? But Brian told her that Lydia was more important right then. She needed simplicity and stability if she were going to get well. She wouldn't be able to teach in Calgary, or in Alberta, for that matter. Rumours of sexual misconduct stick forever.

Eve wonders if being cut off from family and friends is like the blues, a combination of gaiety and sadness. Depends on the family and friends. Both she and Brian travelled in bands for many years. Now she's settled in Vancouver and he here, but even when she and Brian were in the same town, they didn't exactly spend a lot of time together. This is because in their teens, when their parents divorced, Eve and Brian were awarded equally, like assets, one to each parent. Even now, going home for Christmas means going to separate homes. Sometimes they compare notes, each trying to outdo the other: Dad makes more money; Mom has a larger house; Dad gave me front-row tickets to the opera; Mom gave me a car. Whatever. They learned it, probably, from their parents, who were constantly measuring them up against each other: Eve is smarter; Brian is more talented; Eve got a scholarship; Brian won first prize. Whatever. Well, Eve thinks, none of us measured up in the end. Brian is playing two-bit lounges; I'm working in a two-bit music school; Dad's running a two-bit business; and Mom's living a two-bit life. Great. But it doesn't stop them all from trying to impress each other.

After two days here, Eve's main impression is that there's something terribly wrong between Lydia and Brian — the kind of terribly wrong that looks completely normal on the outside. It's to do with interests, or lifestyles, she thinks. Or maybe it's to do with regrets and doubts. Couples all suddenly reversing in midstream, like

Double counterpoint. *When counterpoint is written so that 2 parts can be interchanged, e.g., bass becomes treble and vice versa.*

Whimsical and random. Unexpected. Confusing. Common as dissatisfaction. Half a life to realize what not to do, and the other half trying to undo it. Yin and yang. Lydia now wants to play guitar; she tells Eve and Brian that she has wasted her entire life. She could have been a great musician. Brian sits up for a couple of hours after his gigs, drinking rum, arguing with Lydia about nothing, about everything. Then she goes to bed, usually angry, and he sits at the kitchen table till dawn, studying the advanced mathematics books stacked on top of the fridge. He tells Eve he is discovering prime numbers without the use of computers. "There's no merit to simply punching keys to get the answer," he says. "It's the getting there that counts."

Alligation. *The act of binding together; an arithmetical rule or process for finding the value of a mixture of various ingredients of different qualities and prices.*

Eve and Lydia arrive at Howlin' Joe's a little past 10 p.m. Lydia says she hates going down to see Brian play. "I feel like some kind of groupie," she says. But she sits in the most visible chair in the bar and waves to a number of people, calling out their names above the music. Brian is in the middle of an instrumental; his eyes remain focused on infinity.

"Does he still write songs?" Eve asks Lydia.

"Not so much the past year. I wish he'd get a real job. He could get on down at the docks. Loading or something. It's good enough for other people." Lydia lights a cigarette. "Instead he wastes his time doing that math stuff."

"He isn't just 'other people'," Eve says. "Before he came up here, he was considered one of the top three studio guitarists in the country."

"Yeah. Well. Look at him now." Lydia smirks.

Bitch, Eve thinks. Just how do you think he got here? She waves a waitress to the table and scribbles *Play "All About Eve"* on a cardboard coaster. "Could you take it up to him, please?" she says.

Brian reads the note. Nods. But before he begins playing the request, he scribbles something and whispers to the waitress. She comes back and hands Eve the coaster. On it, she finds the word RE-QUEST.

Quest. *The act of seeking, a search; an expedition or venture in chivalry; the object of such an enterprise.*

Brian took her on her first quest when she was eight. As a birthday present, he gave her a wooden sword (whittled by him), a pot-lid shield, a jar and a green garbage bag suit of armour. Then he told her they had to find a dragon. Eve was ecstatic. She didn't care that dragons didn't exist. If Brian said they did, then she'd find one. They spent the day in the woods behind the school. She followed Brian around, careful and serious. And finally, in the afternoon, when Brian pointed to a garden snake, Eve did not squeal or squirm. She helped him capture it, and carried it in her jar, triumphant as a knight.

Years later, on her twenty-first birthday, Brian phoned and said, "Time for a quest." He brought her a book with a leather binding which read, "All About Eve." Inside were two hundred blank pages of music paper. He took her to his apartment, and for a week they wrote songs together every day. She wrote the lyrics and he the music. She still has the book somewhere. In a trunk, maybe.

She looks up at Brian and smiles. She'd love to take him on a quest now, to journey inside the honeycomb of his head, to help him remember himself. They are similar, she thinks. Music, indispensable, necessary, no matter how much he denies it.

Eve could use a little remembering herself. For the past two years, she has been giving pop voice lessons at MusicVox, in Vancouver. It's a nine-to-fiver; pays the bills. She used to write a lot of songs, too, before Steven. But he's not interested in music, at least not her style of music. He calls blues "old-fashioned." Steven likes New Age. Eve listens to his cds, even though to her they sound like elevator music.

During the last set, while Eve is singing with Brian, a waitress brings them drinks, and points to two enormous men in the audience. Brian downs his rum and Coke in one gulp, then raises the empty glass toward the two men. Eve sips her white wine. The waitress brings Brian another drink. The man in the audience raises his glass and nods at Brian.

"You don't have to drink it," Eve whispers.

"No. But I'm going to." Brian mirrors the gesture.

Eve sings six old standards. It reminds her of the summer they went to Moses Lake, a desert oasis, before her parents' divorce. Mom and Dad paddled around in a canoe all day. Brian and Eve mostly looked for something to do when they weren't swimming. They were ten and fourteen — filled with nervous energy. It's when they started singing together, pretending they were in Las Vegas (the desert helped). Eve made feather boas out of toilet paper; Brian whittled two sticks into microphones. They gave evening performances to their parents, who paid a cover charge, which Brian and Eve spent the next day at the local five-and-dime.

They end the set with "Five Hundred Miles," which they both know is corny, but they're in a sentimental mood. And besides, they probably are five hundred miles away from home.

When they go and sit down, Lydia leans forward and says, "See that fat guy over there? He's been buying me drinks all set."

"Us too," Eve says.

"Maybe he's trying to pick us up," Brian says, and smiles.

Eve grits her teeth and makes an ugly mouth. "Yuck."

"Shhh. He's coming over."

The two men lumber to their table. They each weigh at least

two hundred fifty pounds, and are obviously father and son. The oldest limps. "Good evening," he says in an excessively polite tone. "I'm enjoying your music immensely. May I join you?"

Lydia looks at Brian and smiles. Brian nods and pulls out a chair. Eve frowns, although she understands conventions. You can't accept drinks and not talk. That's what they buy. A few minutes of sympathy. Brian taught her that when they first started playing in a band together. He taught her not to drink, and not to mix. "Booze is running away," he told her. "You run toward something, not away from something." She looks at Brian and Lydia and sighs. Wonders who lowered the standard until it scraped the ground. Wonders, too, why Brian has given up.

"Mike Lemke," the fat man says, leaning forward and wiggling piggy fingers at Eve. "And you are ...?"

Eve looks at Brian, who shakes the outstretched hand. "Brian. My wife, Lydia. And my sister, Eve."

"This is my son, Jordan," Mike says, sitting down.

The young man looks barely old enough to be in a bar. He stares at the ground.

"Go on home, Jordan. Tell your mother I won't be late." Mike dismisses him with a nod, then leans forward.

"Well," Lydia says.

"You have got some fantastic talent," Mike tells Brian, hailing another round of drinks. "And I know what I'm talking about. Columbia Records. You know what I mean? You ought to be recording."

Here it comes, Eve thinks. How many times has she heard this story in clubs and lounges? How many talent scouts, agents, record company executives, managers, etc., etc., can make you a star? The whole damn world can make you a star. All it takes is for you to sit with them on a break and drink. Talk about invertible illusions.

"Excuse me," she says, pushing back her chair.

"Hey, Missy, don't go. You too. You got a mighty fine voice," Mike says.

"Yeah," Eve says and stands up.

Brian scribbles *flam* on her napkin, and grins. Eve squeezes his arm, then hurries to the bathroom.

Flam. *A drum stroke used to mark accent — two notes played very close together.*

The old and-that's-the-punchline Tah-Dah.

When she returns, it appears they're ready to leave, and Mike is going with them. Eve and Lydia walk in front to the car. "What's going on?" Eve asks.

"He's got connections," Lydia whispers. "He might get Brian a recording contract."

Discordant. *A lack of harmony in a combination of notes sounded together; the sounding together of two or more inharmonious or inconclusive notes; a note that is out of harmony with another.*

Here we go, Eve thinks. Where her brother found such an airhead is beyond her conjecture. Why couldn't he have married someone more ... refined? Eve winces. Her mother's words, exactly, when discussing Eve's men.

"I don't think so," she says to Lydia. "I've seen these types. He's a bullshitter."

"You're wrong. Honest." Lydia takes her arm. "You'll see."

On the drive home, there is a full moon. Eve concentrates on the trees, which form sculptures against the sky. Writhing black limbs intertwined. She looks at them through Steven's perspective; tries to measure the unused space. Twelve trees nestled trunk to trunk might fill the expanse of night. Steven has been measuring Eve's apartment. There is something incredibly intimate in his particular attention to details, her details — the number of shelves needed to house all her towels, the width of steps leading to the loft, the position of skylights so she can see the twinkle of stars at night but not have the sun pierce her eyes at dawn. She is not planning to renovate. This is his private construct.

When they arrive home and get out of the car, Mike's limp appears more pronounced. "It's nothing serious," he tells them. "Sympathetic dystrophy." Eve makes a note to look that up in the dictionary.

"Just an old war wound," she mutters under her breath to Brian, who pushes his elbow into her side.

Brian unlocks the door. The babysitter looks up, sleepy, from the couch. "You're home early," she says, looking at her watch.

"Kids okay?" Brian asks, taking out his wallet.

"They're always good." She gets up and puts on her coat.

Brian hands her a twenty. "I'm going to walk her home," he says to Eve, following the babysitter out the door. "She's just a couple of houses down. I'll be right back."

Eve, Lydia and Mike drop their coats on the couch and go into the kitchen. Brian returns in minutes and joins them around the old pine table. Lydia takes out the bottle of rum and pours them all two fingers.

"You have a nice little house here," Mike says. "Reminds me of the house I grew up in. This isn't poverty compared to that. Now *that* was poverty."

"Who said anything about poverty?" Eve says, bristling. It's okay for her to think of them as squalid, she's family. But to let a stranger humiliate them — .

"I didn't mean anything," Mike says quickly.

"Yeah. Sure you didn't." Eve goes to the bathroom, to avoid saying anything else. It's not her house, after all. She locks the door and stares at the wooden counter, the water stains around the toilet. It's pretty desperate, all right. But it is clean. She scrubbed it herself the first day she arrived. It took an entire bottle of Fantastic to coax the dirt off the counters, walls, doors and floor. The shower curtain she threw away.

"This is disgusting," she told Brian. "Can't you see it?"

"It's not so bad," Lydia said. "We're simple folk here, you know, aren't we, Brian?"

Eve looked at Brian. He avoided her glance but said nothing.

"Hey, Bry? Tell her. We're simple folk here, huh?"

"Why don't you clean up some of this mess?" he said suddenly, and Lydia's smile faded. "Eve's right. It is disgusting." And he stomped out of the house.

For the next couple of hours, Lydia wore her frown like a giant V for Victim on her forehead. And she did not help Eve with the cleaning. That was two days ago.

When Eve returns from the bathroom, Mike says, "Hey! Let's drink to Brian's success!" He raises his glass. Brian mirrors him.

Lydia says, "Play 'Blues in the Night,' Brian." She turns to Eve. "It's one of his originals."

Brian goes upstairs to get his songbook and his acoustic guitar. Eve asks him to bring down the dictionary. When he returns, he hands it to her, then settles at the table with the guitar and sings the song. Eve flips pages and puts paper markers in. When Brian is finished singing, Lydia claps enthusiastically. Eve follows, mostly out of courtesy. There's nothing original about it; it's all derivative. Surely Brian knows that. She's written better songs, she thinks.

"What did you think?" Lydia asks Mike. She is leaning forward.

"Okay. Not real recording material though. Too country. You got something else?"

"I think it's a great song," Lydia says, then turns to Brian. "It's a great song, honey. Everybody loves that song. You know how many times they request it at the club."

"So, you work for Columbia Records?" Eve asks, trying to keep the hostility out of her voice.

"Well, not right now, exactly. But I did." Mike shifts in the seat.

"Oh yeah?" Eve sits up. "*When* exactly did you?"

"Well. I worked for them for five years, you know. That's a mighty long time. Get to know the business real good." He holds out his glass. "You want to pour me a little more, honey?" he says to Lydia, who unscrews the lid and pours one for Brian first.

"So when was it?" Eve asks.

"Oh … I'd say … seventeen years ago now."

"You've got to be kidding!" Eve rolls her eyes.

"Of course, since then I've invested my money real good. Got half a million in the market."

Eve gets up and goes to the sink. She pours herself a tall glass of water and drinks it.

"You married?" Mike says, watching her.

"Nope. But you are. Wasn't that your son with you at the bar?"

"Yeah. Jordan," he nods. "Well, you know. There's married and there's married." He stares at Lydia when he says this.

She moves a little closer to Brian. "Play 'Living on Water,' for us honey, would you?" She looks at Mike. "It's always been one of my favourites."

Brian looks down at his book, flips through to find the page. When he begins to sing, Eve closes her eyes, savours the warmth of his voice, the expressiveness of the music. Mom was right, or was it Dad? Brian has a natural talent. Emotions surface at the touch of a string. She looks up at Mike, who is talking about someone he knew when he worked for Columbia Records. Lydia is listening to Brian sing, and clearly ignoring Mike, who doesn't notice. Brian looks up from his lyric book at Eve. He seems embarrassed, she thinks. Or vulnerable. Perhaps it's she who's embarrassed for him.

Perspectives. It reminds her of something Steven did last week, before they went to a movie. He stood against the wall in the hall and asked Eve to mark his height while holding a book on his head at right angles to the wall. Then, he made her stand in the same place, and he measured her.

"You are exactly eight and one-eighth inches shorter than me," he said.

"I'm five-foot-six," Eve said. "You make me sound shorter

than I am." Later, she pulled out her dictionary and looked up the word

> **Measure.** *Means to an end; (Mus) time, pace, the contents of a bar; to determine the extent or quantity, to weigh or judge or estimate by comparison with a definite unit or standard.*

Steven has decided he is the standard by which to measure Eve.

When Brian is finished, Lydia claps, this time not quite as heartily. Mike is still talking, and does not comment or acknowledge the song. Brian takes a gulp of his drink, then begins to play riffs on his guitar, head down, staring at the fretboard. His eyes are soft and pink with alcohol or shame. Why doesn't he tell the jerk off? Eve thinks. Lydia begins to stroke the small of Brian's back. The two of them are leaning toward each other.

Eve rips out a blank sheet of paper from the back of Brian's lyric book and draws a profile in half a page. Then she tries to duplicate the image backwards right beside it. Left brain and right brain functions. She knows that in the second instance, she was not drawing a profile, but imitating and reversing lines through spatial relationship. Sometimes when she and Steven are having dinner with his friends, Eve hears old melodies within their words. She sang them herself once, when the feeling was genuine. She stops herself from commenting. Wariness and weariness have no place in your twenties, Eve thinks, when the future stretches before you like an apple tree in blossom; when you still believe all you need to do is pick the fruit you want; when you don't worry about ladders and falling and worms and pesticides.

"... So this guy was working with the top people in the business," Mike is saying. "And believe me, he knew. Why, if it wasn't for him, I wouldn't have three-quarters of a million dollars growing for me in the stock market. You know what I mean?"

"What do you do?" Eve says, abrupt.

"Right now?"

"Yeah. Seventeen years is a long time. You still in the business?"

"Well. Not exactly. I mean, I still know people. But I've been selling franchises the last few years."

"What? You mean record stores?" Lydia's brow furls.

"Pizza franchises."

Eve laughs. Not a humorous laugh, but a sarcastic one. "I guess you meet record people all the time, huh?" she says.

Brian looks up and winks at her. This makes her feel a million times better.

"Well. Quite frankly," Mike says, "I haven't heard anything yet that I think is record material."

Lydia reaches for Brian's lyric book and flips through several pages. Her movements are jerky and quick. She licks her finger on every page turn. "Here," she says, smiling at Brian. "Play this one. I love this one." She strokes the back of his neck.

While Brian is singing, Mike goes to the washroom.

"Let's get rid of him," Eve says while he's gone. "We don't need this shit."

"Aw, let him be. He's just a pathetic old man," Brian says.

Lydia puts her arms around him and kisses his cheek. He turns his head and kisses her lips. Eve looks away, but she's thinking about Steven.

Contiguous. Meeting so as to touch; adjoining, neighbouring.
Contiguity. Contact; proximity in time or space; (Psych) the immediate relation of two impressions, a principle of association.

Have they proximity in time or space? It is impossible to judge the distance in their thinking. A few days ago, Steven told her that her name is an incomplete version of his. "Man," Eve answered, "is an incomplete version of woman." He did not see the absurdity. And when he scowled, she added, "*Woe* man," exaggerating the "o." And still, he couldn't see the humour. In fact, didn't call for three days. An ego wound, she thought. Self-inflicted. It only reaffirmed her belief in the power of shared pasts. The reference points through which lines are drawn. Eve and her friends have many dissecting lines: they've been married, separated, divorced; they've backpacked, hitchhiked, driven, flown across the country, the continents; they have come to understand the inner workings of things in a similar way. Their stories echo each other's memories, like old, familiar songs.

Lydia and Brian are necking at the table. Eve finds this very confusing, as if she has misread signs all week.

When Mike returns from the bathroom, he is limping considerably more than he did earlier.

"What's the matter with your leg, anyway?" Lydia says.

Eve hears a subtle change in Lydia's voice. A hint of irritation, like a small gust passing.

"It's pretty bad," Mike says. "Sympathetic dystrophy." He makes a great show of sitting down.

Eve picks up the dictionary on the table and turns to one of her marked pages. "It's not in here," she says. "But I see **dys:** *bad,* *badly, depraved.* And **trophic**: *deranged nutrition due to nervous disorder.* Now, what do you suppose that means?"

"You know, they might even have to cut off my leg," Mike says, seriously.

"Maybe it's **trophy**, as in sports," Lydia says. Both she and Eve begin to giggle.

"There's nothing funny about losing your leg, you know," Mike says.

"No. It's more like *careless*," Eve says, and she and Lydia burst into new laughter.

Brian begins singing a new song, drowns all sound. And slowly, they all become silent, stare into their glasses. It is as if the music demands dignity. It swirls around them and rounds the edges.

"I never heard that one before," Lydia says, her voice both accusing and frightened.

Lydia doesn't want Brian to succeed, Eve thinks suddenly. She's afraid to lose him.

She watches them, perplexed. Brian looks at Lydia, and his eyes communicate something so private and binding between them that Eve feels tears well in her eyes. He knows.

> *Harmony. The just adaptation of parts to each other, so as to form a complete, symmetrical or pleasing whole; the agreeable combination of simultaneous sounds, music; concord or agreement in views, sentiment, etc.*

Before Eve, Steven went out with a seventeen-year-old. "She was nine years younger than me," he said, as if the two disparities could bond them. In music, it is the different sounds which, played together, form harmony. The doubling of one voice is unison.

"Play 'Wild Blue,'" Lydia says, and Brian begins the familiar intro. For once, Mike keeps quiet. He stares at his drink and sighs.

When the song is over, Lydia and Brian smile at each other. She squeezes his arm. Eve gets up and goes to the washroom.

When she returns, Mike says, "You married?"

"We've been through that one already." Eve sighs.

"You know," Mike says, "I've done a lot of traveling. I meet a lot of women. Gets lonely on the road. You know what I mean?" He winks.

"So, what is your tie to the music business now?" Eve asks.

Mike shifts, and the chair squeaks. "You know, Gordon Lightfoot was a personal friend of mine. I helped make him who he is."

"So why are you selling pizza franchises?" Lydia's voice is clearly hostile.

"I got almost a million dollars invested in the stock market, you know."

"Yeah. And growing by the minute." Lydia gets up.

"You got a good figure, you know, for someone who's had kids," Mike tells her. "I know. I've been with a few married ladies." He winks at Brian.

"I'm tired of this," Lydia says, looking at Brian.

Brian leans forward, halfway across the table. "What the hell do you want?" he says to Mike suddenly, his voice knifelike.

Mike sits up, uncertain. Eve, too, is confused/fascinated by the sudden power shift. It is as if she is watching a nature program on TV. Mike looks down. In the animal world, eye contact equals challenge. Brian's gaze does not leave Mike's face. Lydia is stroking Brian's arm.

"Well ..." Mike says.

"Get the hell out of my house," Brian says. He is completely still, but Eve can see the coil of a cougar, perhaps.

They are all silent. Expectation is a tight winding of nerves. Mike gets up and hobbles out of the kitchen, dragging his leg. They hear him stop in the living room to get his coat. Then the front door opens and shuts.

Eve gets up and goes to the window. She watches Mike walk up the street until he becomes one of the hunched shadows. Tree ghosts in the moonlight. It would make a good title, she thinks. When she gets home, she'll rent some recording equipment. She can afford it. There are a lot of songs waiting in her head.

She looks back into the kitchen where Lydia is pouring Brian another drink.

"Do you think he'll be okay?" Lydia says.

"He'll get a cab at any street corner. This is a drinking town. Don't you worry about him." Brian lifts his glass. "To us," he says, and downs it in one gulp.

Da capo. *'From the head,' to go back to the beginning and start again.*

Isosceles triangle. *Having two sides equal.*

"Why did you ask me to come?" Eve says to Brian.

Lydia and Brian watch her, but they don't say anything.

"I'm going home in the morning," Eve says. As she goes up the stairs, she thinks maybe she'll take a few days driving down. Stop at a few small towns along the way. Flea markets and garage sales. Who knows what treasures she could find. She pauses at the top of the stairs, listening.

Lydia says, "Honey, play 'Starlight' for me."

Fugue

Fugue (from L. *fuga,* flight): a polyphonic composition based on a theme (subject) which is stated at the beginning in one voice part alone, is imitated by other voices in close succession, and reappears throughout the piece at various places. Usually in three parts called Expositions: 1st Exposition consists of *Subject* and *Answer*; 2nd Exposition of *Antecedent* and *Consequent;* 3rd Exposition of *Dux* and *Comes.* Intermingled, are *Episodes*: short sections in which the subject is not being stated in any voice parts.

1st Exposition:

SUBJECT: Marianne lies awake, listening to Joe's even breathing, her eyes watching the green digitals marking minutes. She turns onto her stomach, pulling one edge of the blanket over her head.

"What's wrong?" Joe lifts his head. She can feel it in the movement of the sheets.

She comes up from under the covers; sees his face soft with sleep in the dawn light. "Nothing." She lies a couple of minutes longer, then slides out of the bed.

"You okay?" he asks.

"Just can't sleep, that's all. I'll go read awhile."

She watches him settle back into the pillow, then tiptoes out and pulls the door shut behind her.

She does not go directly to her book, or to anywhere in particular. Wanders through the rooms, barefoot, long cotton nightgown — a ghost searching, she's not sure what. Perhaps the solid reminders that she has lived here — still lives here. There are bits of her spread everywhere.

Outside, it is summer. Birds awaken to an inner clock; she hears the first chirps. The cat yawns on the couch, perks up her ears. Marianne strokes her whiskers, watches her stretch and head for the cat door. She wishes she could keep the cat from hunting, but she knows about instinct.

Marianne stands at the window and stares past the balcony, at the tree shapes in the backyard. Dark creatures, limbs outlined in the lightening sky. Above, the clouds a reddish hue. A storm, perhaps, she thinks. So the saying goes. She shivers, turns into the kitchen to make coffee, then goes to the basement to the music room. It's at the opposite end of the house from the bedroom, so she can play the piano whenever she wants without disturbing Joe.

ANSWER: For many months now, she has been restless. She has fought the feeling — something she can't describe, or perhaps chooses not to describe even to herself. She surrounds herself with normalcy, with the mundane rituals of everyday life. Sometimes, when she can't control the thoughts, when they begin to scratch and burrow in her mind, she seeks the solace of music. She has been learning to play a Bach fugue — "flight" the dictionary defines "fugue." She finds flight in the concentration and discipline required to play the piece; manages to keep the thoughts from nesting.

Episode 1:

"Joe is wonderful," she often tells her friend Clelie. "All a woman could want." In her stomach, a tightening. Is she trying to convince Clelie or herself? "We're equal partners. He doesn't expect me to do things for him." She pauses, then adds, "Although I'm not entirely selfish." Why does she say this? Selfish. What is being selfish? Not doing things for someone? Marianne's mother thinks Marianne is selfish.

"You have to make him feel like a man and he'll be one."

A man needs a woman to be a man? Marianne shakes her head. The responsibility too great. She'll never understand her mother.

Hey little girl comb your hair, fix your makeup,
Soon he will open the door...

"Don't point out other beautiful women. He's likely to make comparisons."

Christ, Marianne thinks. If she listens to her mother, to the ads, to the constant bombardment of what she's supposed to be, she's likely to forget who she is. She tells her mother this.

"You've got to please a man to keep a man." Aphorisms. Her mother has one for everything. Especially on the subject of men. Marianne doesn't want to keep a man. She sees no point in it. Keep a pet. Keep a garden. Keep a diary. Never a man.

"You're too selfish," her mother says. "You'll lose him." Back to that word, filled with its negative connotations. Lose an earring. Lose a game. Lose an hour. Marianne is trying to define selfish. She's trying to justify her and Joe together. They're well suited. They don't argue, don't shout. They're comfortable. What more could she want?

2nd Exposition:

ANTECEDENT: She is drawn back to the window by scuffling noises on the balcony. The cat has returned triumphant, a small mole in her mouth. Marianne opens the back door, pulls shut the screen before the cat can come in. She panics for a moment, goes toward the bedroom to get Joe.

"What is it?"

"The cat's got a mole on the balcony."

"Shut the screen."

"I did. But I can't stand the thought of it being tortured out there. Can't you come and take it away from her?"

"Leave it alone. It's probably injured anyway."

"But what if it isn't?" She leans in the doorway.

"You can't change nature. Forget about it." He turns over, away from her.

She shuts the door quietly and tiptoes back to the window. She feels her own hunger tighten her stomach. The mole runs, twelve steps to the cat's two, struggles for a moment as the cat's teeth sink gently into its flesh, then lies still. Marianne watches, horrified, fascinated by the clear instincts — hunter and hunted — each playing a delicate role. She watches the hunter, becomes one with her in the intricate dance.

CONSEQUENT: Marianne thinks back to when she first met Joe, to those years when he struck a chord inside her, harmonious as the white and black keys she presses on the piano. She wishes she could have locked the two of them in a perfect cadence. Dominant and tonic. Even in music, she thinks, nothing is equal. Complements. White and black keys. Natural and accidentals. Dominant and tonic.

Marianne opens the door and stamps her feet hard against the wooden balcony floor. The cat looks up startled, drops the mole, who scurries to the edge of the balcony, hides behind a post. The cat's claws cannot reach; she lies, yawns, stretches her paw, touches the tail. Marianne goes back inside and watches from the window. The mole huddles against the edge. If only he'd jump, she thinks, he'd be safe in the tall grass below, in the burrows beneath the fresh mounds she sees each day. She imagines his family tunneling an escape route. He's too frightened, like her.

Episode 2:

Clelie has been telling Marianne that she has broken off with her live-in mate "because of stupid, insignificant differences."

"That's the way it usually is," Marianne says. "Two people tend to agree on the major issues. Or they wouldn't have gotten together in the first place. It seems to be the idiosyncrasies that ruin a relationship." She says these things to Clelie as if she believes them. She is becoming like her mother.

Slowly, over months, years, Marianne has noticed more and more disparity in views between her and Joe. How did it happen? She thought they were so alike. When and who changed? She doesn't think herself so different — perhaps more cynical, more realistic than she used to be, but her principles, her integrity, her compassion are unchanged.

"You're too tolerant," Joe says to her when she talks about injustices. The girl across the street is twenty-four, on welfare, has four children and is unmarried. "A burden on the system," Joe says and Marianne argues.

"It could be you. It could be me. Would you have them homeless?"

"It wouldn't be you or me," he says, "because we have more sense than that."

"This has nothing to do with sense," Marianne says. "We've simply had more privileges. Opportunities."

"Everyone has equal opportunities. The problem is this government."

"*We're* the government," she argues. "Do you have a better solution?"

They never resolve these conflicts. They simply agree to disagree.

Episode 3:

"It's easy for you," Clelie tells Marianne. "You have emasculated Joe."

Marianne bites her lip, rolls her eyes. Pointless, too, she realizes, to try and explain to Clelie how she feels. How does one take away masculinity or femininity? Are they just labels that can be ripped off? Or masks or makeup that can be removed so easily? She cannot imagine being stripped of what makes her a woman. She says to Clelie, "What you're saying is that there is no such thing as equality. That two people can only be equal if one surrenders his or her being to the other."

Clelie shakes her head. "It's human nature. We're divided into hunters and hunted."

Episode 4:

Marianne imagines this. She's in the basement room, in an airport, waiting for Joe to complete the cadence. It is not a perfect cadence until both chords come together in succession, dominant and tonic. They know each other too well. She's sitting at a small round corner booth in the airport lounge, half hoping he won't see her if he does come. She can see planes from here — sleek metallic birds, or submarines, missiles, she can't make up her mind what. She's been staring at the book in her hand for the past twenty minutes without turning a page. Sartre's *Nausea*. No matter how hard she tries to understand the words, they don't make sense. She begins rereading at the top of the page:

A perfect day to turn in upon oneself; these cold rays which the

sun projects like a pitiless judgement on all creatures enter into
me through my eyes ...

She tries to imagine the sun cold, icy as packed snow. Snowblind. Reflections. The hard glare of the plate-glass windows. She watches Joe approach in the mirror image — a cold imprint on glass; watches the rectangle of light — his ghost — a crisp photograph lozenged across the table; feels herself drawn into the glare. She skids onto the surface. White, hard, unyielding. Her antithesis. She draws strength in the rigidity of schedules, cloistered habits, safe, familiar. They live together. Joe and her. Man and woman. Woman and man. Individuals, strangers, friends, lovers. Time has puttied all the scratches, the cracks, the voids, the lacerations, gaping mouths — all smooth and even. She leans her face on the hardness of white, colourless as she feels, her insides puttied smooth. Only her nails bleed, covering white moons, scarlet drops bouncing off the impermeable surface.

His hand is on her shoulder, pulling her back. His shadow falls across the glare, that mirror through which she sees her place. She has matured into this new instinct, and mustn't allow herself to fall into the old familiar yearning, elusive as the glint on wet teeth.

3rd Exposition:

DUX: Marianne pulls on a dressing gown, boots, and descends the stairs to the garden. Below the balcony she reaches for a rake, then pushes it gently along the edge, to urge the mole to safety. He does not understand her gesture. "I'm trying to help you," she says. "Jump." The mole is as frightened of her as of the cat, caught between hunter and rescuer, without knowing the difference. From below, she can see the soft pink pads of the cat's paw moving along the edge. She tries once more. The mole scurries into the cat's claws.

COMES: They play with each other. She and Joe. Cat and mouse. Roles constantly reversing. When things are too settled, too pat between them, she extends her claws. A little. Just enough to make him stop, look back; just enough for her to take a closer step. She bites him gently, tightens the grip only if he struggles. She feels the warmth of him in her mouth, the quivering of his heart on the tip of her tongue. She lets him go, afraid to crush him.

Joe says, "You just can't stand it when things are smooth, can you? I can always tell when you're going to get into one of these moods."

"I can't help it," Marianne says.

"You've always got to wreck things. You should try using your energy positively. You waste far too much of it trying to find something wrong."

"If I could find something positive to think about, I would," Marianne says, more for dramatic effect than anything. She waits, poised.

"Well, if you're so unhappy, why don't you leave?"

Marianne watches Joe's eyes, cat slits. She lies limp. "I'm just depressed, that's all. Can't I even get depressed without you giving me ultimatums?"

They end these sessions in bed where Marianne can lose herself in the struggle of their bodies, one against the other. And later, she's never sure who won.

Cadence:

Marianne stomps up the stairs to the balcony. "Let him go." She growls at the cat, the two of them enemies. The mole lies limp between teeth. She chases the cat, frightening her, frightening them both, until she drops the mole. Marianne watches it run to the edge, scurry back and forth over the long drop. She pushes the rake against its tiny legs, forces it over. She looks through the railing. Instead of heading to the safety of the grass, the mole runs under the balcony. Hides among planks and the discarded evidence of her and Joe's life.

Marianne goes down with the rake, making noise, trying to scare it away. She lifts planks, kicks her feet hard against anything, everything. The cat follows her down, lazy. She stretches on the grass and waits. Marianne and the cat, two sides of the same thing.

"You keep watch," Marianne says to the cat, finally, when it appears she'll never find the mole. She goes back upstairs to dress.

When she returns and peers over the balcony, the cat is lying very still — only her head moves, left to right to left to right. Marianne imagines she can see the whiskers twitching.

Throughout the day, Marianne often returns to the balcony window.

Joe says, "Don't worry. The cat'll get it eventually."

What if it doesn't? Marianne thinks. What if the cat gets too tired, too lazy, loses interest? What then? The mole is below at the edge of her boundaries. She wanted him alive in his own ground. What if he settles out there, among her things, what if he slowly moves into her house, her bed?

At nine-thirty, Marianne feels the delicate web of dusk begin to weave. Joe is out. She sits by the window, keeping watch. Finally, she can stand it no more. She goes down to the garden. The cat is flat on her stomach, paws stretched out; she appears to be sleeping. Only her eyes are open — green fluorescent moons.

"Come here," Marianne says. "I'm going to help you." She begins to lift the planks. The cat sits up, comes to rub against her leg. "You show me. Where is it?" she whispers, the two of them conspirators. She continues to displace things — boxes, gardening tools, deck chairs — gingerly, afraid to find the mole. Suddenly, the cat perks her ears, rubs her nose along the length of two planks leaning into each other. Marianne jumps back, heart pounding. She reaches for the rake and scrapes it along one side of the wood. The cat follows the scent back and forth. He is there, settling among her things. Marianne takes a deep breath. Her hand trembles as she lifts one of the planks, exposes him, and watches him run into the cat's soft palate.

Rondeau

Rondeau: a form of instrumental music in which the opening section recurs, alternating with different sections called couplets (*ABACADAEA* etc.)

A: The first indication we had of Molly's strange behaviour came the afternoon she arrived late at the Hospital Ladies Auxiliary meeting and didn't even say, "Excuse me," or tell us what had detained her. Anna stopped speaking and waited for Molly to take her place before passing her the Minutes, which she, as Secretary, should have been recording. Molly read the first page quickly, then looked up and said, "What the hell are you all staring at?" Just like that. Anna cleared her throat twice, the way she does when she disapproves of something. I glanced around the table. Susan was fingering the bangles on her wrist, clinking them together in a rhythmic metallic sound; Liz sorted her papers, then straightened the edges by slapping the pile against the table; the others were pretending to read the agenda. We all avoided looking at Molly, who was wearing a pair of black jeans, the stretch type that leaves nothing to the imagination, and a floppy T-shirt with a neckline wide enough for a shoulder. Clothes that probably belonged to her teenage daughter who we knew was seeing a young man from across the river (with no objections from Molly).

Don't get me wrong. I have nothing against looking young, or wearing jeans, especially if you've got the figure for it. And Molly does. We were surprised, that's all. Molly's wardrobe had always consisted of Laura Ashley dresses — paisleys and prints with little crocheted collars and buttons up to the jaw, no matter what the occasion.

We waited while Molly fished for her pen in the large African straw bag, then resumed the meeting as if things were normal. Several times, Anna raised her eyebrow at me and I shrugged. When we adjourned and were supposed to go to Molly's house for cake and coffee (we do it on rotation each week), Molly got up and said, "See you next week, ladies," and sauntered out, casual as can be. We were so surprised, I don't think anyone spoke for a minute. It was not like Molly to forget her responsibilities. In the end, we decided to go to Anna's, who lives two doors down from Molly, and we noticed Molly's car wasn't in the drive. And somebody, I'm not sure who it was, made some comment about Molly and Father Bryce.

Now, I'm not one to judge people without knowing the facts,

so I said, "There's a lot going on at the church this time of year."

"And I bet none of it's religious," Susan said.

B COUPLET: If Molly's husband, Lawrence, had not been wrongly diagnosed as having cancer, Molly would not have gradually transformed into someone we could no longer understand. At first, when Molly believed Lawrence wasn't going to get well, she barricaded herself in her bedroom. Closed blinds and prescription tranquilizers. So we decided we had to do something. We went to see her one afternoon, and explained how selfish she was being. After all, it was Lawrence who was dying. We didn't put it so bluntly, of course. But it was true. Molly seemed to be only concerned with what was going to happen to her after Lawrence was gone. Soon afterwards, she began to forget to return our calls; sometimes she'd have no cream for the afternoon coffee; often she'd miss our Tuesday bridge nights without cancelling. We excused her these lapses, knowing how upset and concerned she was about Lawrence. Then, she started attending Catholic services at St. Thomas's on the east riverside. Not just on Sundays, but almost every day.

A few months and a battery of tests later, we discovered Lawrence's doctor had made a mistake. And if he hadn't been Susan's husband, I'm sure he'd have found himself in a malpractice suit. But I figure, nobody's perfect; everyone is entitled to one mistake. Lawrence was put on medi-cation, and he returned to normal. But Molly did not.

A: And then, there was that other time? About two weeks after the Auxiliary meeting. It was Saturday night and my turn to have the party and, it being near Halloween, I asked everyone to come in costume. We were all there and Molly and Lawrence were late, and we were wondering what they'd wear, when the doorbell rang and Lawrence walked in, without Molly, dressed as a priest. Nobody laughed, you know? Being too embarrassed. And then Lawrence announced, "I've come as Father Bryce," and started laughing. Naturally we all laughed too, though it sounded to me more as if we were laughing at him, not with him. And nobody asked where Molly was.

C COUPLET: On two different occasions, I tried to talk to Molly about it.

The first time occurred when we still thought Lawrence was going to die. Molly was constantly at the church and, in our opinion, neglecting Lawrence.

"It makes no sense," I said to her, trying to appeal to her reason. "How could you possibly believe in the existence of a God who can do this to your husband?"

Molly hesitated. Then she said, "Father Bryce —"

"I don't give a damn what Father Bryce says. I asked what you believe."

"I believe what I'm doing is right."

"I think you're wasting your time," I told her. "You'll never forgive yourself if Lawrence —"

"Shut up," she said, and covered her ears.

The second time was months later, when we had all stopped pretending that Molly's church-going had anything to do with religion.

"You should be spending more time with Lawrence," I told her.

"This thing has gotten out of hand."

"It's my business," Molly said.

"It's everybody's business now. You must realize the whole town is talking."

"Let them talk," Molly said.

"What about Lawrence? Think about him."

"He's my business too."

"You're infatuated with Father Bryce," I told her. "The ultimate unattainable love."

Molly scowled. "This has nothing to do with romantic love. I'm helping God. I'm helping the church." And she would say no more.

A: And then there was another incident. We heard that Molly was going for a weeklong horseback-riding trip with Father Bryce and Father Connelly. On a ranch in Alberta. Molly'd never been on a horse, as far as we knew. So I phoned her a couple of days before her departure. "Lawrence tells me you're off on a trip," I said.

"Horseback riding."

When I realized she wasn't going to add anything, I said, "You could have told us."

"You seem to know already," she said.

"We might not have had a fourth for bridge. If Lawrence hadn't told us."

"Well, he did."

And that was that. So, at bridge the next night, I had nothing to tell the girls that they didn't already know.

I invited Lawrence to dinner while Molly was gone. He and Dan are partners in the law firm. They're also best friends.

"So," I said to Lawrence when we'd finished dinner. "Why didn't you go horseback riding?"

"She didn't ask me," Lawrence said, and gave me one of his sardonic smiles. "Besides, I wouldn't have gone if she had."

"I don't think it's right," I said. "And if you ask me, you should put your foot down."

"I didn't ask you," Lawrence said.

The week passed slowly, Anna or one of the others calling every day to ask if I'd heard anything. They knew Lawrence would probably tell me. Since this thing began, he has treated it like one big joke. Trouble is, the joke's on him.

And then, we heard Molly was back, from Anna this time, because the car was in the drive two days earlier than we expected. So I called Molly and asked, "How was the trip?" and she said, "Great," and talked for about ten minutes and it was almost as if we were best friends again. And finally, I said, "If you were having such a good time, how come you cut your trip short?"

And she said, "Father Connelly fell off his horse and broke his neck."

"My God, Molly. Is he all right?"

"He died instantly," she said.

Just like that. As if it were a triviality she forgot to include in the story. Naturally I phoned Anna immediately and told her the news. And Anna said, "You don't think they did it, do you?"

"Of course I don't think they did it. It was a terrible accident, that's all," I said. "Poor Molly's devastated. She could hardly talk to me over the phone."

That afternoon, at the coffee clan, the girls said, "Well, maybe it's for the best. Nothing like a tragedy to bring people to their senses." And, over the next few days, we all decided Molly was obviously going through a midlife crisis and, having scraped through her ordeal, would surely need all our help. Not so different from when we thought Lawrence was seriously ill and not expected to live past a few months. Of course, then Molly was a true tragic figure. She walked stoically among us, the future widow withstanding all adversity. In my opinion, Lawrence's recovery was so anticlimactic, it catapulted Molly directly into the arms of the Catholic church. And Father Bryce was there to catch her. She converted last year. Since then, she has spent most of her days at the church, has had Father Bryce to dinner at least four times a week (Anna told us) and, according to Lawrence, offers him the best Scotch in the house, which Father Bryce accepts liberally.

Before the next Hospital Ladies Auxiliary meeting, I cautioned the girls, "Don't anybody mention Father Connelly. She really is too upset," me being worried about what Molly might say, and wanting to protect her.

D COUPLET: Molly used to be a good wife, a good mother, a good hostess. She fit in, you know? She was very organized and meticulous. The type of person who keeps an appointment calendar and checks it every day, who makes lists, is never late, goes shopping once every two weeks, dragging two carts through the aisles, and never forgets anything. We had good reason to worry about her.

In the middle of this, Dan was exhibiting signs of stress — short temper, insomnia, a few drinks too many at night — and needed my support. He had been appointed to defend two policemen who had picked up a drunk and thrown him in jail overnight. The next day, the man was found dead in his cell and people claimed he hadn't been drunk at all, but having a heart attack. Dan told me that although everyone is entitled to a defence, he didn't like taking this case one bit. So I said, the man's been drunk every day of his life, so if he didn't happen to be on this one night, well, how is a person to know?

A: And then there was the weekend when Lawrence was at a conference in Vancouver and Father Bryce's car was parked in Molly's drive from Friday night to Sunday morning. When I called to warn her that people had noticed and were starting to talk, she said Father Bryce had lent it to her. Naturally, it seemed right when Anna suggested it, that I be the one to call the Bishop, being Molly's best friend and all.

E COUPLET: I don't like to say it exactly, but if it weren't for me, there'd be a lot of trouble in this town. I've done my best to help friends and strangers alike. Take the time, for instance, that Susan was stopped outside Blair's Jewellery Store by a salesgirl who claimed Susan had stolen a gold bangle. Imagine. Susan, whose husband could afford ten of them. Susan offered to pay for it immediately, but the salesgirl insisted she'd stolen it. Susan phoned me from the shop and when I arrived, the salesgirl was threatening to call the police and the store owner. Fortunately, I recognized her as the daughter of someone Dan defended in an ICBC claim. So I calmed her down by reminding her who I was and said surely Susan was only guilty of an unfortunate oversight. The girl became sullen, then she said yes, perhaps she'd jumped to conclusions, and, of course it must all be a mistake. Susan returned the bangle and since then, she and I have cautioned people not to shop there because you can't trust a salesgirl who clearly overreacts.

Or the time two years ago when the new male teacher was hired at the high school. Joe Stanley was his name. All the women liked him, teachers and students alike. We invited him up to the house — just to see for ourselves — and before an hour was up, he was criticizing our town, and how City Hall was doing nothing to build housing for poor people. And when I suggested those poor people could get themselves jobs, he became outraged and very rudely called me a fascist. In my own home, too. And I, being a School Trustee, voiced my opinions very strongly at the next meeting. And before you know it, Mr. Joe Stanley was relieved of his position.

A: A couple of Saturdays after Lawrence returned from Vancouver, we were at Molly's for the weekly party, and two days had passed since I'd called the Bishop. It was a difficult call, because I couldn't accuse them of anything specific, not knowing the facts. What I did say was that I had good cause to be worried. Not just me, mind you. Everybody knows; they don't talk about it openly, but it's the looks in their eyes that give them away. And when the Bishop asked my name, I said I was a "concerned parishioner." But he said these were serious allegations upon which he could not act unless I identified myself. So I said I was a spokesperson for the Ladies Auxiliary, but in the end, I gave him my name, in confidence, of course.

Well, there we were, in the middle of dinner and the phone rang and Molly picked it up in the hall, and then she said, "Hold on.

I'll take it in the bedroom." And she told Lawrence to hang up as soon as she'd got it, which he did. And he rolled his eyes and made the sign of the cross, so we all knew it was Father Bryce.

Molly didn't come back for twenty-five minutes. I know, because I kept checking my watch. When she did return, she looked awful, eyes red and makeup running. She didn't sit down. No. She stood at the head of the table, pointed straight at me and said, "You did this. How could you?" And everybody stopped talking, naturally, and looked surprised, though none of us women were.

Then Lawrence said, very calmly, "Sit down, Molly."

And she shouted at him too. "How could you? You probably put them up to it." Then she ran out of the room, into the bedroom and slammed the door behind her.

Everybody stared down at their plates, until Lawrence said, "Excuse me," and followed Molly into the bedroom, only he didn't slam the door.

And then Dan demanded to know what was going on, and I had to tell him and the rest of the men. When I'd finished, Anna cleared her throat twice and said, "Somebody had to do it."

On the way home later, Dan, who's normally a very mild-mannered person, turned to me and said, "Damn you. Why couldn't you mind your own business?" I tried to explain that I made the call because Molly was my friend and if she was unaware that she was ruining her reputation and her marriage, I wasn't. People in a small town will tolerate eccentric behaviour for a short period only, and Molly's had been going on too long.

"Gossip," Dan said. "That's all it is and that's all you do."

I didn't talk to him for two days, and I made him get his own dinner too. The only reason I resumed speaking to him is that I had to know the facts. Dan finally told me that Father Bryce was being transferred to another town. I called Anna immediately and she said, "Molly's going to need us now, more than ever. We've got to help her through this." And we thought, wouldn't it be nice if we could all get in a car and go away for a weekend, like we used to do? Shop all day and sit up all night talking in a hotel room as if we were kids back in college, telling each other secrets. Only we couldn't decide who should phone Molly and suggest it.

Molly stopped coming to the meetings and I didn't call her. Not because I did anything wrong, but simply because I didn't want to upset her. Lawrence turned down dinner invitations and Dan wouldn't tell me anything. So, you see, we did all we could to help Molly, and we had no way of knowing she would take all those pills.

F COUPLET: Six months have passed. We still get together three, four times a week, for meetings, coffee clan and bridge nights. At first, when Molly was in the hospital and Lawrence was trying to buy a law practice somewhere, we were all uncomfortable with each other. It wasn't anything we talked about, but rather it was evident in the silences and in the way one of us always tried to fill them. A forced gaiety, perhaps.

Two weeks ago, Molly and Lawrence moved to Kelowna. Susan told me she heard that's where Father Bryce was transferred, but who can believe in gossip? Anyway, I finally felt it was over. As if their leaving had erased the oppressive gloom that has been settled among us these last few months, and which we have been unwilling to acknowledge openly.

A: Dan has a new partner, Bob, in the law firm. His wife, Irene, plays bridge and is anxious to involve herself in the community. It's the best way to meet like-minded people and make good friends. This afternoon, we invited her to our coffee clan. She's a little younger than we are, but I think she'll fit right in. When Anna pointed out that women in our position must be examples to the people in this town, Irene squirmed and pulled her skirt over her knees.

Snake

When he had to, Joshua carried the snake around his waist, hidden by a sports jacket a couple of sizes too big. He had an enormous beer gut already, so it wasn't hard to imagine six more inches. This is how Mandy met him, seated in a nightclub. The snake's tail formed an erect penis between Joshua's legs. Mandy, who was not afraid of snakes or penises, reached out and squeezed it.

The snake constricted, and Joshua took in a sudden breath, which Mandy mistook for heightened passion. She invited Joshua to her apartment. By the time she realized her mistake, they were in bed, the snake between them, around them. She was never sure if it was

Joshua or the snake's tail that entered her. Naturally, when she got pregnant, she wondered if her baby would be born with black horns. Sometimes, in the night, she thought she felt a trident push against her stomach walls.

The baby's birth was uneventful, as was the baby himself. A pudgy, pink mound of flesh, a fish-mouth, and every orifice bleeding seeping leaking fluid. The snake, on the other hand, curled itself in front of the mirror, its skin cool and dry as sin.

Cry Wolf

White wolves, the CBC announcer says, packs of them. Marauding wolves with famished eyes and pitiless snouts. They're quartering your dogs, your cats, devouring them within the village limits. We've closed the schools, the pool hall, the church and that empty shack where kids go to smoke and drink and sniff. We've locked the children out so you can lock them in, save them from grappling teeth.

The children in the Arctic village don hockey clothes and congregate at the edge of town, clear off a square and skate round and round, back and forth, sticks to the ground, oblivious to the ice-grey eyes of a pack of wolves camouflaged in snow.

(A pack, like cigarettes, perhaps, white, slender, or soldiers on board an aircraft carrier, ordered at attention, white uniforms, brass buttons glittering like greedy eyes. Later, they'll slip into camouflage gear, board their planes and land on a foreign shore, guns raised, the hair on their arms bristling with fear.)

These wolves, the announcer says, are defending/extending territory, dismantling boundaries, tracking children, glory and *the pursuit of happiness*, starved for the buffalo meat on the other side of the garage wall, for the dismembered bodies everywhere, severed heads, bleached antlers, wide gaping eyes. These wolves, he says, are dangerous. Don't be misled by their delicate faces, their kaleidoscope eyes circling a makeshift arena in the Arctic, foreign ground, the hair on their backs bristling.

Fear

When the knock comes, Elena hides in the closet. Her husband, Richard, peers through the peephole. "It's only the paper boy," he says, but Elena slides the closet door shut. She turns on a flashlight and locks herself in. On the back wall of the closet, she has tacked a large travel poster — a sun setting over water, palm silhouettes; in the foreground, a young couple holding hands on the beach, her long white dress slit up the side to expose a tanned, perfectly shaped leg. Were they ever like this, she and Richard? She imagines their faces over the ones in the poster, the large letters M-E-X-I-C-O stencilled across their calves.

The closet is small enough to hide in, and large enough to live in, she thinks, ear to the door, almost expecting to hear S-L-A-S-H, S-L-A-S-H sounds, like premonitions, like shrill commands forcing her to act.

Knock, knock, a shallow sound against the hollow wooden door. *Knock, knock*, and it's the tinny sound of knuckles rapping at the motorhome door.

"Don't answer it," she calls out. "Don't answer!" and closes her eyes. She huddles in one corner, turns off the flashlight and covers her ears, all the while hearing the *slash, slash, slash* of a knife cutting her husband's face, his arms, his chest. She hears the drawer slide out, the pistol cock, the shots — *bang, bang, bang, bang* — surprisingly loud. Then they're all right, aren't they? Richard bleeding and frightened, Elena's knees wobbly, her hands trembling around the pistol.

Knock, knock, knock. Again. She scrunches into an invisible ball in a corner of the closet. The air salty, the sand smattered in blood.

"It's only the paper boy," Richard says, his voice against the closet door. "Elena, open up."

But she is back in M-E-X-I-C-O, three years ago, and her hand will forever be firing a pistol in response to a knock late at night. The two men with their savage eyes and TV-desperado faces, fat stubby fingers forcing open the door.

"Open up," Richard says. "For God's sake, Elena, it's only the paper boy." He rattles the closet door, and she scrambles around in the dark, searching for the right drawer.

15 Love

She wakes up one morning and there, right beside her house, she sees a man wedged between a boulder and a large rock in front of a side door to the Vancouver Tennis Club.

He is crouched in an unlikely position, his head lopped far too low against his chest, his legs splayed at unnatural angles. She goes outside in her dressing gown and calls to him from the porch. But all she can hear is the *whack, whack, whack* of tennis balls. Next door, there is an underground tennis court which she can see now and then, when the side door is open.

(She only gets a glimpse, of course, before the custodians quickly block her view. The green subterranean turf evokes

Greek and Roman mythology — a secret garden beneath the city, perhaps, where beautiful deities frolic in their brilliant whites, thighs glistening with sweat.)

(In winter, the sunken court more closely resembles a table hockey game, its players small toy figurines she could almost manipulate with a twist of the wrist.)

Another drunk, she thinks. Lately, five homeless men have taken over the park next to the tennis club, an irony which does not escape her. She often steps over them midday, on her way to post a letter or buy lettuce, over their empty bottles that glitter like zirconia in the sun.

One day, the homeless man (or she hopes it was him) called to her as she crossed the park, and asked if she'd like to hear a poem he had written.

She stopped, smiled.

The homeless man recited a four-line Hallmark sentiment, replete with red roses, blue violets and a strong Jesus connection. He beamed at her. She said, "Terrific. Fabulous." She said, "Thank you," and walked on, thinking *sad, pathetic*, thinking *what can I do?* Of course she did nothing.

(The homeless man wedged between a rock and a hard place is not a poet, a seer, a prophet, or a romantic of any kind. He is not drunk, not sleeping, not up or down on pharmaceuticals; he is not contemplating life or recalling his childhood; he is not summoning power or seeking his inner child; he is not meditating and he is definitely not praying. The homeless man wedged between a rock and a hard place is dead.)

He died last night, leaning against the newly painted green of the Vancouver Tennis Club, his ear against the wall, trying to imagine what kind of life would induce people to dress up in white costumes and bat green fluorescent balls at each other, furiously and repeatedly, as if they were afraid to speak, as if each mighty *whack* were a blow inflicted, a hostility carefully aimed, as if it hadn't occurred to them to save the $10,000-a-year membership and have an argument instead.

Whack, whack, whack, whack. Like a rug being aired out, a marriage slapped, a screen door slamming in the wind.

To fall onto a knife blade is silent, the skin and flesh easily accommodating a sharp object, almost welcoming it. To fall on the blade at the precise angle to split your heart is a little more difficult, but can be achieved with practice. In the darkness, the blood is like water and drips easily into the grass, seeps into the ground, along the lead piping of the heating ducts leading into the ceiling of the subterranean tennis court where well-to-do, muscled middle-aged men and taut-skinned women play tennis below, and suddenly discover large fat drops of blood splattering down on them through the light fixtures, coagulating on the pleats of their tennis skirts, on the polo collars of their white shirts.

"It's raining blood outside," one might note, voice steady, backhand vicious.

An opponent might shrug. "Another war. Who can keep up?" drilling back a winner.

15 love, 30 love, while up above ground, the sky is a cobalt darkness even the dead can't escape.

Lost & Found

A woman, at Vancouver Airport, Departures, her feet squished into black pumps, rectangular body, thin long neck craning this way and that. She exudes the acrid, acid smell of anxiety, that middle-of-the-night sharp awakening, sweat-drenched and unknowing.

She gets up in a panic, whispers that she has lost her sense of direction, her humour, her parents, her husband. Ticket agents and airport personnel direct her left, right, straight ahead, turn, circle, as if she will find them all neatly stacked in an inner room. Lost & Found. She wonders if she is the one lost — a skier out-of-bounds — if she should sit still and let others find her. A wind swirls in her ear: put one foot in front of the other, but there is only a precipice.

She leaves the airport, gets in her car and drives toward the East-West Connector, named perhaps to encourage relations. A neutral zone, she thinks, peace. Halfway, she parks her car at the side of the highway and walks into the bog.

In her purse: tissues, pen, lipstick, face powder, hand mirror, black gloves — tidy fossils, generic life — then, a paperback with its front cover ripped off. She flips the pages, a blizzard of memories flies out and dissipates in the air around her. Everything lost, she thinks. Everyone gone so gradually, she hasn't noticed until now that she is eighty-two years old, and there is no one to call.

For a full week, passersby see the car, orange numbers scrawled on the rear window like a cryptic message, a secret handshake. No one imagines the woman dead in a bog beside the road, skin like the page of a paperback. No one turns her into a screenplay, with long-lost grief-stricken relatives who blame the government for not checking up on her, who blame her doctors for not prescribing antidepressants, who blame her for not having the decency to die in her own bed, at their convenience, her life and death echoing in their ears like a premonition.

Hungers

I. Versions

WHEN I WAS TWO, MY SISTER MARCIA, WHO WAS THREE AND A half, lifted me up over a balcony railing and held me upside down by the ankles suspended two storeys above the street. When my mother walked into the room and saw this, she slipped off her shoes, took a deep breath and held it, then slowly crossed to the balcony so as not to startle Marcia.

Depending on my mother's mood, this part of the story is more or less elaborate. Sometimes she is wearing high heels (blue, to match her dress); other times Chinese red brocade slippers (and doesn't take them off); sometimes she is wearing black laced boots that would take too long to remove, so she has to walk on tiptoe very very slowly and carefully. The distance varies too: eight steps, fifteen, twenty-five. Sometimes, and this when she's feeling particularly dramatic, she is coming home from a friend's or the train station, and sees me from below. Then she must climb the stairs (often she can't find her key immediately and doesn't want to ring the bell in case Marcia is distracted).

The story always ends with my mother grabbing my ankles the exact moment Marcia lets go of them. And then, my mother leans back and says, "The trouble with Marcia is that she was so jealous," implying that Marcia's entire life has been one enormous mistake (this being the first) made up of escalating small ones. A little like a novel, perhaps, though Marcia doesn't think of it in these terms.

WHEN MARCIA TELLS THIS STORY, IT IS ALMOST IDENTICAL BUT for two things: the intent and the ending. She says there was a parade that day moving below the window and I was too small to see over the balcony. I cried, waving my arms in the air. Marcia was watching the multicoloured floats of tissue-paper flowers while hopping wildly from foot to foot to the rhythm of marching bands. She pointed and pointed but I was just too small. Then she had an idea (sometimes, she attributes this idea to one of the passing floats — the three bears sitting on small chairs or the elephant perched on its hind legs on a box). She went inside, dragged the piano stool to the balcony and lifted me onto it. Then she stood on it herself, and carefully hauled me over the railing. Here, the versions coincide, although Marcia always stresses the fact that she never let go of my ankles, in fact, was annoyed at my aunt for pulling me back before I could see the giant blue float with the yellow ducks on it. She's certain it was my aunt, and not my mother, of whom she has no recollection until years later. She always ends the story with, "The trouble with Mother is that she keeps trying to fit herself into other people's pasts," like a new character who shows up in a rewrite but who nobody recognizes.

WHEN MY AUNT TELLS ME THE STORY, SHE IS LYING ON HER bed in Italy, in a darkened room, shutters tight against the August heat, and I am reclined on a pink chaise lounge smoking Canadian cigarettes. She recalls the minutest details, which imply that her story is the real one, or perhaps that she has the best imagination. For example, she says it was the 13th of August and she was wearing her black dress with the tiny blue flowers and the V-neck. We had all returned recently from our weekly visit to the cemetery where Marcia had thrown a tantrum when she wasn't allowed to pull all the petals off all the flowers. (My aunt had been widowed two years, she tells me). In order to appease Marcia, who was still crying, she took us upstairs to the balcony to watch the parade. After twenty minutes or so, she carried out the piano stool because her arms were aching from holding me up to the railing. She says Marcia was restless, thirsty; she had thrown her hat into the street and was now wailing and pointing to it as it wafted down.

My aunt gets up and goes to the kitchen, while I light another cigarette and push butts to one side of the ashtray. She returns with two glasses of orange juice and soda and lies back down on the bed. I have not seen her for twenty years and am anxious for her to fill the spaces in my memory, to confirm or deny, although why I should believe her version, I don't know.

She says she only left the balcony for a few moments. She doesn't place blame or justify her actions, although she does tell me it was not easy looking after two little girls at her age.

The rest of the story coincides with Marcia's and this relieves me because two people surely couldn't invent the same details.

I DON'T RECALL THE INCIDENT, ALTHOUGH THROUGH HEARING it, I've memorized the balcony and my position on it. I even imagine I can recall the people on the street at the time, although here logic fails me and when I retell this story, it is many years later and the balcony is on the twenty-eighth floor of a Vancouver apartment building. I am there with Harris, or Andrew, or some other English name. He is my lover of some weeks and it is his birthday. This story always occurs at night, downtown, when I can imagine the Vancouver skyline and the ships anchored in the harbour.

In the story, we've had a fabulous dinner — steak and lobster (flown in from the East Coast) — then Harris has blindfolded me (black silk scarf — implying ritual) to prepare me for a surprise. He leads me to the balcony door and slides it open. I feel the warm summer air and hear tires on wet pavement below, although it is August and it hasn't rained for thirty-six days. Harris urges me over the sill onto the balcony, and walks behind me, his arms around my waist until a certain moment when he tells me to stop. Here, the details vary, according to my mood. Sometimes only his fingers touch my waist; other times I am leaning back against him and laughing. Either he removes the blindfold or I reach back and undo the knot. The moment I can see, however, the versions merge.

Harris has removed the balcony railing, and I am balanced precariously at the edge.

How long I stand there depends on the reaction of my audience. Then, Harris slowly pulls me back to the safety of the sliding glass door which feels solid even though I can see through it. I try to end the story here, by saying, "The trouble with me is that I'm too trusting," thereby absolving Marcia of all guilt, although she doesn't appear in this story.

More often than not, however, I am pestered into giving a denouement, when we all know some stories are best left at the climax. I vary these too. Sometimes I run out of the apartment forgetting my shoes and car keys and have to buzz Harris and go back up and retrieve them; other times I slap him across the face, square my shoulders and leave in a most dignified manner; other times I push him hard and he lands with his head over the edge of the abyss and begs for mercy. With this ending, I say, "The trouble with Harris is that he underestimated me," when actually it wasn't Harris at all, but my mother who keeps pushing me to the edge by restructuring my past until I'm unbalanced and can't trust my own memories.

WHEN MY FATHER TELLS THIS STORY, HE SETS IT IN LONDON, England (where he was at the time), on a foggy, grey day (probably to reconcile setting and content). He has just finished the first page of a letter to my aunt (my mother is with him), when he hears the cry of a child outside his window. He throws open the balcony doors in time to see a small girl holding a baby by its ankles over the railing of a balcony above. The girl is crying, "I can't hold her any more," and the baby is shrieking. Here, my father says he distinctly recognized those voices as Marcia's and mine. My father climbs the outside of his balcony railing, secures his feet into the rod ironwork and holds out his arms. Sometimes the balcony is concrete and he straddles it and has to lean into the street; other times it is wooden and rickety and he has to balance carefully to keep it from toppling. Often he is fully dressed because he is expecting an important visitor; occasionally he has just come out of the shower and is wearing only a towel. Below, a circle of people hold up the edges of a blanket or sometimes, the street is deserted. The ending, however, is always the same: the girl drops the baby, which my father catches without incident. He ends this story with, "The trouble with children is that they have no concept of danger," which is true, considering how Marcia and I keep perching on the edge of a balcony, watching memories which shift dangerously from narrator to narrator and before I know it, I can't tell fact from fiction any more, and this is really dangerous because it implies that my life, the one I am trying to live so accurately, can and will be distorted, reordered, adjusted, and will emerge, years later, as a piece of fiction in some stranger's living room.

NOW PHOTOGRAPHS. YES, THEY TELL A MORE PRECISE STORY. Here's a family classic. In the middle of evergreens is a large tree with a thick branch on which my mother, Marcia and I are all standing, crushed against each other. We are smiling, and wearing identical puffy dresses in pastels, with frilly crinolines underneath. My mother's mouth is especially beautiful; the crimson lipstick accentuates the whiteness of her teeth. Each of us is hugging the tree trunk or each other with one arm, and waving with the other to my father who is taking the picture. You have to look close to see that Marcia is wearing track shoes and she is standing on one of my mother's bare feet.

II. The Savage God

I'M WAITING IN MY ROOM, READING, WHEN MY OLDER SISTER, Marcia, comes home. I watch from my upstairs window. Marcia sits in the front seat of the car, staring straight ahead. My father goes around and opens her door.

"Claire, come down this minute," my mother calls, her voice tremulous.

I shut the book, check myself in the mirror and go down. My mother, Eclipse — as she now calls herself — is moving around the room, fingering this and that, as if Marcia were an important guest rather than her seventeen-year-old runaway daughter who's been on her own the past year, living à la Plath, trying to turn dying into an art. We've all been to counseling, so this time, there are no hysterical outbursts, no appropriation of guilt, and no barrels of tears.

In the hall, Marcia stands, impassive, features gaunt, skin sallow. Can't weigh more than ninety pounds, I think. Marcia is wearing a white shirt tucked into blue jeans. Despite the cropped lime-green hair, the thirteen silver rings in her ears, she looks fragile, like pictures I've seen of holocaust victims.

I glance at my mother. Eclipse-ex-Betty plunges her hands into her skirt pockets. She's a psychologist by profession, but since she quit work three years ago, she's been devouring New Age theory, seeing a therapist once a week, and obsessively searching for herself, in my opinion, in all the wrong places. She is wearing a benign smile. "You look wonderful, honey," she says. "Welcome home."

"Hi, Marcia." I try not to stare at the bandaged wrists. I lean forward and kiss her cheek; don't know where to touch her.

Eclipse waves us into the living room. There are new rugs and drapes for Marcia to see. She sustains a barrier of chatter. "Your room is all ready. You're going to love it," she says. "Or do you want to sit down here? Dad, take Marcia's bag upstairs. Do you want to freshen up, dear? Can I get you a cup of coffee? Claire, don't just stand there. Go and make the coffee, for God's sake ..." Marcia's face is an empty reservoir. She goes through the motions Eclipse suggests, until finally, she is in her room, asleep.

I return to reading all about suicide because, at home, it's a taboo subject. The disturbing or unpleasant is dealt with in silence. In a crisis, my parents oversimplify: "Separation," they might say, or "Death," as if by speaking in the abstract, they can distance the problem. Suicide is an abstraction, I think, fantasized immortality. I wish I could ask my parents why Marcia's like she is or whether there's something we could have done or should be doing to make her happy. I wish I could ask my parents many questions and get answers instead of definitions detached from meaning. For example, before Marcia came home, Eclipse called me in to discuss *habituation.*

"Forming a new habit involves a process called conditioning," she said, without giving me context for this piece of information. Then, she went on to explain Pavlov's experiment, and ended with, "Thus he was able to induce salivation in the dogs merely by sounding the bell." She smiled, and I knew this was the end of the lecture. Later, I heard my dad tell Eclipse that cocaine was really easy to get if you had money or were pretty.

A light knock, then Eclipse comes into my bedroom and shuts the door. "Claire, you've got to promise," she whispers. "I don't want you asking Marcia about suicide, you hear?"

Suicide fallacy: Those who attempt suicide once never do it again. Four years ago, the first time, I asked Marcia whether she had gone through a dark tunnel toward God or something. Instead of answering, Marcia started wailing, and I was banished to my room, grounded for a week. The counselor at school told me I had become a scapegoat for the family's guilt. I looked that up: *scapegoat,* "in ancient Hebrew rites, the goat sent into the wilderness on the Day of Atonement after sins of people had been placed on its back by the High Priest."

Eclipse is waiting by the door, impatient. Perhaps she's worried I will ask her a direct question, like *Why does Marcia want to die?* Instead, I say, "I won't ask her. Don't worry."

The first time Marcia took all those pills was three months after our father moved in with one of his students.

"A bimbette," Marcia said. "Look that up."

"Good riddance. We don't need a man in this house," Mom said. She hadn't renamed herself yet.

We were all so angry, none of us knew what to do. Marcia spent

nights at her boyfriend's house; Eclipse scoured New Age book-
stores and returned with dozens of self-help manifestos; I loitered
at the mall after school with a pack of runaways. Often Marcia
would come and take me home, where she and Eclipse would lock
into a tremendous argument about Eclipse's inadequacy as a mother.
Even I could read the subtext. Our father drove up some weekends, and we all tried to pretend things were normal. Eclipse
coped by forming serial attachments to some group or other, some
"community" or "family." I stopped asking questions. Now and
then, Eclipse would follow me and Marcia around the house, her
eyes like blindfolds, her face smiling like those women's in a movie
I saw on TV — *The Stepford Wives* — only they weren't really
women, but robots the men had fabricated to their specifications.
And I wondered if anyone ever thought to make a movie called *The
Stepford Parents* — and in this one, kids could have the perfect Mom
and Dad, whatever that is.

At the hospital, Marcia stared at the ceiling, silent. When she
did finally start talking, she told me she wasn't going to live past
twenty. I told my parents. Dad said things like "fantasy" and
"romanticism." Eclipse said things like "craving attention" and
"paternal rejection." I understood it perfectly. Why would Marcia
want to be old and sick and wrinkled, when she could die young
and glamorous in a satin slip like Marilyn Monroe? *Suicide fallacy:
The old are serene in death*. I'd seen my grandfather thrash in his final
days. Besides, suicide sounded romantic. Artists did it: Vincent van
Gogh, Virginia Woolf, Anne Sexton, Jimi Hendrix, Janis Joplin,
Sylvia Plath and three generations of Hemingways, to name a few.

MARCIA'S BEEN CRYING FOR THE PAST HOUR, LIKE SHE DOES every night. She's been home two weeks already, and hasn't come out of her room except to go to the bathroom. We take meals up to her, and Dad has moved in a TV, to which Marcia appears indifferent. After school, I sit with her and read trash novels out loud, but I'm terrified to ask Marcia anything, in case I upset her. In my room, I read about suicide ... *An escape from painful circumstances or an act of revenge on another person who is blamed for the suffering that led* ... Is it me? I want to ask.

I considered it myself, seriously, last summer, after Eclipse's *mystical experience*. I would come home to strangers in monk robes, to erected altars and screechy voices singing eerie Druid songs, to "Everything's fine. Stand still. The forest knows where you are. Stand still and let the forest find you." It made me want to be a tree disease, an exterminator of all these smug enlightened faces. It made me desperately crave the mother of my childhood. One day, I packed my gym bag and left, but not before I demolished every altar in the house. Eclipse followed me around, wringing her hands, saying, "Claire, calm down. Claire, we are all one." My father (who had returned home as casually as if he'd been on sabbatical) said things like "repressed rage," and "hostility," which was closer to how I felt. I slammed out of the house, shouting, "Fuck you. Fuck you all." Downtown, I sat on the pavement on Granville Street, trying to prove wrong the suicide fallacy: *Those who threaten to kill themselves never do,* and wondering how long it would hurt if I ran in front of a passing car. I considered other possibilities: pills would make me choke on my own vomit; hanging would asphyxiate me or break my neck; falling out of a building could give me a heart attack, depending on the height. I stayed two nights — dodging policemen, do-gooders, drunks and addicts — and, in the end, decided death was not an option.

I STAND OUTSIDE MARCIA'S ROOM AND KNOCK QUIETLY, SO AS not to wake our parents. "Marcia?" I whisper. "It's Claire."

Marcia's sniffling stops for a moment. Then, "What?"

I turn the knob and enter. The room is bathed in the bluish glow of the TV which flickers in shadows across Marcia's face. Marcia looks at me, then reaches for a Kleenex and blows her nose. I begin to sit on a chair, but Marcia moves over and motions me onto the bed.

"Are you okay?" I ask, although I can clearly see she isn't.

"Not so loud," Marcia says. "I don't want the whole damn family in here." She wipes her eyes on a corner of the sheet, and smiles.

I put my arms around her, and we hold each other tight, like we haven't for years. I'm crying too, but I'm not sure why. Perhaps relief that Marcia's back.

After a bit, Marcia pushes me away. "You've got to help me get out of here," she says.

"Why?" I ask, for lack of anything better. The psychologist has not prepared me for this.

"They're never going to leave me alone. I feel like a prisoner."

"They're worried about you. We all are." We've been told that Marcia might try to do it again. Eclipse and Dad have taken everything sharp out of the room, removed all the belts. I can't sleep nights, worrying Marcia might be dead.

"It was an accident, Claire. I didn't try to kill myself. Why doesn't anyone believe me?"

I want so badly for Marcia to be all right. "I believe you," I say.

Marcia smiles, her face suddenly radiant. "You and me, Claire. We'll get the hell out of here. Drive down the freeway. Windows open." She shuts her eyes and breathes deeply. "Can you smell it? The forest and the air? Everything's black and beautiful and there's just the two of us."

"Where would we go?"

"What does it matter? It'll be an adventure. Come on." She sits up and slides out of bed.

"Marcia, the doctor—"

"Screw the doctor. He's just trying to make a buck."

Next thing, we're in Dad's car, and Marcia's driving west on Highway 1, toward Hope. The windows are down and our jackets zipped up because it's late September. Between us, we have $22.45 and Marcia's Visa card (one of those extra issues for family members, because Eclipse and Dad figure Marcia should be able to come home no matter where she is). The radio's blasting and we're bellowing along with it, shrieking with laughter. Everything is funny. At night, the freeway is endless, unconfined. Free-way. We pretend we're driving on the rim of the world. One false turn and we'll plunge into eternity.

I reach across to Marcia and take her hand, careful not to touch the scabs on her wrists. When we were little, the two of us were inseparable. We played together, slept together, guarded each other's secrets and concealed each other's lies. *What happened? When did it change?* Marcia told me she has no memories, that there's no point to remembering. The books say that the suicide puts a full stop on life, and that this requires a severing of the past, but I can't imagine Marcia cutting me out of her heart.

We drive for a while, holding hands, singing out, while our hair flies out the windows and the wind drowns out our words. And for a bit, I feel we are truly back together again, truly happy.

When we hit the Harrison Lake turnoff, Marcia slips her hand out of mine and signals.

"Where are we going?" I ask, turning down the radio.

"You'll see." She smiles at me quick.

I shrug. We drive past Agassiz and into Harrison. Even in the dark, I recognize it, or perhaps I'm reconstructing a memory — four years ago, Marcia and Mom and Dad and I in this car, approaching the lakefront, picnic basket full, hats and swimsuits and towels and air mattresses bulging in the trunk. Marcia kept sticking my doll out the window and calling her "Hurricane Barbie." We were laughing wildly while Dad said things like "hysteria" and "impulsive behaviour," and Eclipse said things like "adolescence" and "hormones."

Marcia takes a couple of turns and stops in front of a small secluded cottage. She shuts off the engine and the radio. It is breathlessly quiet.

"Have you ever lost someone you loved deeply?" she asks in the darkness.

You, I think. But I say, "Is that what's happened? Is all this about a man?"

Suicide fallacy: that suicide and young love are inextricably tied. Romeo and Juliet, passion and romance. Truth is, statistics show the highest rate of successful suicide occurs in people between fifty-five and sixty-five. The young are more numerous only in their attempts.

Marcia sighs. "You're too young, Claire. You just don't understand."

"Some man leaves you and this gives you the right to ruin our lives."

"It's not about losing the man," she says. "It's about losing the love."

"I love you, Marcia. And Eclipse and Dad —"

"I know." She sighs. "I know." She pats my hand, then opens her car door. "Wait here," she says. "We're picking up my friend, Jamie. He's got a little something for us." She winks.

I wait in the car until they return. Jamie slides past the steering wheel, sets himself in the middle, between me and Marcia, who begins to drive again.

"Claire, this is Jamie," she says.

"So, you're Marcia's little sister, huh?" He laughs and holds out his hand. I take it, although I don't like the intimate tone of his voice. He looks a little older, twenty-two, twenty-three. Not like the boys at school.

"You leave her alone," Marcia says. Then to me, "Don't mind him. He's okay. He's my best friend."

"I wasn't worried," I say.

Jamie laughs and spreads his arms along the back of the seat, as if Marcia and I are his dates, his fingers touching both our shoulders. We turn right at the beach, go past hotels and motels. It's 1:30 a.m.; the lakefront is deserted. At the end, Marcia turns left onto a narrow road which skirts the shore. I wonder what secrets lie hidden in those lake-front homes. Are there suicides even there? It reminds me of the Solar Temple deaths — that immaculate million-dollar mansion filled with the decomposing bodies of people who believed they'd be transported to a UFO. Their deaths, a frivolous act. Hedonistic. Perhaps, I think, they're inside Valhalla, the Vikings' paradise, to which admission was a violent death. Or in the Land of Day, the paradise of the Iglulik who believed if you died of natural causes, you were condemned to eternal claustrophobia in the Narrow Land. Nothing unusual about this hunger for early paradise. I shake my head.

"Close your eyes," Marcia says. "And don't open them till I tell you."

When I next open my eyes, everything is black. Marcia has shut off the headlights. At the exact moment when I might panic, the moon expands and I can see. "Spooky, huh?" Marcia says. We all laugh. Soon, she steers left into a lane, still without using headlights. She turns off the radio and rolls up the windows. We drive until we come to a dark house facing the lake. "Here we are," she says, shutting off the engine. "Let's move the seat back."

Jamie takes a packet of coke out of his inner jacket pocket, puts it on the dash and proceeds to make lines with a razor blade. *Cocaine, a white, crystalline drug, stimulates the cortex of the brain, producing euphoria.* "I read somewhere," I say, "that cocaine destroys the body's ability to produce endorphins."

"Endor-what?" Jamie asks.

"You know. It's what makes you feel good."

"Try a bit of this. Guaranteed to make you feel good." Jamie winks at me.

"They have drugs now," I say, tentative. "So you don't have to feel bad all the time."

Marcia laughs. "You just stick to your books and let me pick the drugs, okay?"

That's what I'm afraid of, but I don't say so. I look at the big deserted mansion beside them. "Whose house is this?" I ask.

"Friends of mine," Jamie says. "They're only here summers. Some weekends if the weather's good. It's okay. They don't mind us being here."

I don't believe the part about them being his friends. Not for a minute. Marcia's acting really restless. "Hurry up," she keeps saying, as if she can't wait to do whatever is next. Finally, the lines are ready and I watch them do four apiece. I sniff a couple myself, just so they don't think I'm a baby. It makes my teeth want to clench together, like having three espressos in a short time.

"We're going down to the boat now. You've got to be completely silent, Claire. Not a sound, or else we'll leave you here." The urgency in Marcia's voice makes me anxious and breathless. But I go along with them.

They untie the boat and take the oars. "Jump in," Marcia whispers.

"I need a life jacket," I say. "Are there any life jackets?"

Marcia jumps in and Jamie begins to push the boat.

"Marcia, I can't swim. You know that. I need a life jacket."

"Get in or stay behind."

I can't see Marcia's face in the dark. I step into the boat. Then Jamie jumps in, puts out the oars, and begins to row. Marcia holds her finger in front of her lips.

We row out and down the lake, past shorefront cottages and houses. All are dark and seem uninhabited. When we have passed the last house and the Provincial Park campground, Jamie drops the motor into the water and starts it. We begin to head up the lake. "We did it!" Marcia says, standing up so that the boat sways side to side.

I hang on.

"Ace!" Jamie says, then turns to me. "Come on, little sister. Want to go for a swim?"

"Let her be."

"Hey, I'm only kidding. Here. You take the steering wheel." He lets go of it and fishes in his jacket pocket again. "I brought along a bit of smoke. Cuts the edge." He starts rolling a joint, and I take the steering wheel, although I have no idea where we're going.

Marcia and Jamie smoke two joints. I pass on both, and keep staring straight ahead. We're quiet now, into our private thoughts. Marcia looks vulnerable, bent into herself. What the hell do the psychologists know about my sister? *Negative self-concept.* *"Bad me" complex. Manipulative. Impatient. Frustrated. Restless.* I looked them all up, and they're still just words. *Manic depression.* Does my wonderful sister, Marcia, really believe she's helpless, worthless, insecure? Dad says things like "immature" and "intolerant." Eclipse says things like "withdrawn" and "rebellious." *A predisposition genetically transmitted.* I wonder where Marcia's devils come from, and if you can be born like this. An accident of nature.

"So, what happened?" I ask Marcia, who looks up, puzzled. "Your wrists. You said it was an accident."

Marcia shrugs.

"Marcia's gonna be okay," Jamie says, putting his arm around Marcia's shoulder.

What does he know about her? I think. He hasn't lived in our house, hasn't seen Marcia locked in her room, or in a hospital bed unable to recognize anyone. He hasn't seen the cuts in her arms, the bathtub full of blood. "How the hell do you know she's going to be okay?" I shout.

"Stay cool," Jamie says. He turns to Marcia. "Why did you bring her, anyway?"

"Why did you bring him, is more like it," I say.

"Leave your sister alone. She's had a rough time," Jamie says.

"Fuck you," I say.

Marcia sits up, as if she is coming out of a trance. "Hey. We're here to have a good time, aren't we? I'm all right, Claire. Really I am." She stands up and dances a couple of steps. The boat sways. I hear water splash against the sides.

"Marcia, don't."

"Look what else I got." Jamie pulls a mickey of whiskey out of his jacket. "Here, have some. It'll cool you out."

Marcia reaches for the bottle, tips it back and swallows. I yank the mickey out of her hand and hurl it into the lake. Marcia erupts into laughter, loud and strange. She pushes me aside, slides into my seat and grabs the steering wheel. Jamie begins to laugh too, and I'm forgotten. Marcia pushes the throttle, and the boat picks up speed. I hang on tight.

"Marcia, slow down," I say.

"What the hell are you worried about? Didn't I say we'd feel the wind in our hair? We've only just begun." She leans forward and I hear the acceleration; imagine Marcia's hand jamming the throttle, her open mouth, her half-crazed eyes.

"Slow down, damn you. You're going to kill us."

But Marcia doesn't. "Fuck, Claire. I can't believe you're my sister, you're such a suck."

Jamie laughs and laughs. He is standing in the boat, hanging on to both sides.

"Sit down!" I yell. "You're going to turn us over! Marcia, slow down, please. Marcia. I can't swim."

"You don't understand," Marcia says. "We're invincible." Before I can stop her, she abandons the controls and climbs over the windshield. "Whoooeeee!" she shouts, teetering on the fibre-glass top, her arms spread out like Christ on a cross.

My heart is beating so hard, I think it will burst out of me. I grab the steering wheel, but it's dark and the only thing I can see clearly is Marcia's silhouette in front of me, shifting, erratic. What do the books know about my sister? None of the fancy phrases make sense to me now. *Suicide is prepared within the silence of the heart, as is a great work of art.* The possibility of Marcia's death is not art. We are somewhere in the middle of the lake. Marcia and Jamie are careening out of control at either ends of the boat, and I can't swim. I try not to think of this, my eyes straining to see deadheads, islands, anything we might strike, but it is too dark and we are traveling too fast.

"Come on!" Marcia shouts. "Come on up here and taste the freedom!" She leans forward, obstructing what little vision there is. "Come on, Claire. Can't you see? We're invincible!" She shifts her weight from foot to foot.

The boat lurches drunkenly.

Jamie shouts, "Fuuuuuuuck!" Then a loud splash in the roar of the motor.

The boat is still accelerating. "Marcia!" I plead. "He's gone over! Marcia, please, get in the boat."

Marcia can't hear me. I wave my arms and point behind me. I'm afraid to pull back the throttle, afraid any change will topple Marcia, send her flying into the darkness. Marcia does a manic dance in front of me, as if tempting fate. Then, she suddenly flings herself against the windshield, hauls herself over and collapses into the seat beside me, panting madly. The boat is still traveling at full speed, and I'm clinging to the steering wheel as if it were a life preserver.

"We've got to go back," I say, my voice high-pitched.

Marcia begins to make a sound in the back of her throat, a wail, a growl, something eerie and inhuman. I'm terrified I have lost her forever.

"Hang on, Marcia," I say, again and again. My reflexes pull back the throttle, and turn us around. Where to look? How to find Jamie in this darkness? I begin to circle a small area. Round and round. Call Jamie's name and slowly, hesitantly, Marcia joins in until we are both calling in unison, pleading, as if we are praying, only no god is listening. I look over the edge at the black expanse of water, so threatening and so inviting, and for a moment at least, I think I understand Marcia, constantly running from everyone, from herself.

"He's gone," Marcia says, suddenly. I sense the change in her: a calm — silent and unnerving. Marcia leans across and eases the throttle back. She pries my fingers off the steering wheel and I begin to cry. My hands and knees shake violently. Marcia is fully composed. She gently slides me out from behind the wheel and trades places with me. I huddle in my seat.

Marcia reaches across and pats my hand. "Claire, I'm sorry."

I continue to cry. "We've got to go for help. We've got to get someone."

"It's too late," Marcia says. "There's nothing we can do."

"They'll bring a rescue boat ... He might be swimming out there — ."

"We're going to put the boat back and go home. You can't tell anyone. Do you understand?" Marcia's voice is flat, unemotional. This Marcia is as frightening as the wild one.

"No, I don't understand."

"Don't you see? They'll send me away."

"It wasn't your fault," I say. "It was an accident."

"They'll send me away anyway. I'd rather die."

"I'll tell them the truth," I say, though I know Marcia's right. I stare at the strip of black water between mountains. "We can run away," I say. "You and me. Together. I'll look after you, Marcia."

Marcia turns to me then, breathless, bright-eyed. "Yes, yes," she says. "Together." She pulls me into a tight embrace. "Close your eyes and don't open them till I say."

The boat sways. I keep my eyes shut and think about the Aztecs, about those willing youths who climbed the temple steps, even though they knew they'd have their living hearts cut out.

III. Family Reunion

"FOR CHRISTSAKES, MARCIA," MOM-EX-ECLIPSE-ALIAS-BETTY says, "why do you insist on wearing those horrid track shoes?"

"They're comfortable," Marcia says.

"But they're so *unbecoming*."

"Hiya, Claire," Marcia says to me. "Been here long?" She gives me a quick hug and, holding on to my arm, she pushes her right toe against the heel of her left shoe and slips her foot out.

"A couple of hours," I say.

"You alone?" she asks, looking down the empty hall.

"Yes."

Marcia nods, then kicks off her second shoe; sends it flying against the wall.

"You wouldn't catch me dead in these," Mom says, gingerly picking up Marcia's runners and setting them perfectly evenly to one side.

"I'm not trying to impress anyone," Marcia says. "If people don't like them, tough. I'm happy in them."

I smile. Marcia never addresses Mom directly when contradicting her.

"Betty, let's not start something in the hallway," Dad says, including himself in this skirmish, although he hasn't a thing to do with it. "Marcia's only just arrived."

"I'm not starting anything," Mom says. "I was just making a comment. She can wear anything she likes. It's her life."

Marcia's husband, Charles, pushes against the front door and enters, staggering under the weight of a large suitcase. "That's it," he says. "Everything's in." He takes off his shoes and follows us into the living room.

It's another Christmas when the whole damn family congregates at 2595 West 33rd Avenue in Vancouver, for two days of quarrels, accusations, shouts and tears. It's an annual family ritual in which pasts are dug up and examined; partners are dissected and scrutinized, financial conditions are compared; bitter disputes resurface from other years and continue with renewed vigour; secrets are disclosed, usually someone else's, because in this family nothing is sacred or unshared. We unlock our suitcases and willingly display every piece of dirty underwear. Then we fight over who bought it, who owns it, who stained it, who cleaned it, and who watched. And, of course, the worst thing that can happen and inevitably does, is that someone brings out the family photo album, and this reminds us of unresolved animosities which, no matter how distant they are in the past, suddenly become the cause of all that is wrong in the present.

Right now, seven of us form the core of these visits: myself, Mom, Dad, Marcia, Charles, and Uncle Dan and his wife, Lucille, who we never call "aunt" because she's four years younger than me. Over the years, I have brought one husband and two live-in mates. Nobody cares about this except Lucille, who always finds a way to show her disapproval. But she tolerates me probably because this isn't her house and my life is none of her business (as Marcia has told her on several occasions).

Despite what I've said or perhaps because of it, none of us would miss this reunion. We all bring cameras and snap-snap-snap, then mail each other copies of the photos which fill new pages in the album and fuel new feuds the following year.

We are all scattered around the province. Marcia and Charles live in Penticton, a town in the interior known for its orchards and pensioners. They own two hardware stores which keep them pretty busy. Sometimes they camper to Palo Alto or Vegas, and never invite any of us (not that we'd go if they did). Uncle Dan and Lucille live in Kitimat, a northern company town of about ten thousand and shrinking. Mom and Dad have been up to see them on several occasions, but I've only been there once, for their wedding four years ago. I live in Vancouver, and although everyone has to fly through here to get to anywhere else, none of them call when they're in town.

In the living room, we find Lucille watching a soap opera and Uncle Dan talking on the phone.

"For Christsakes, Dan, Marcia's here," Mom says. "Can't you just forget business? It's Christmas."

Uncle Dan waves his free arm to shush her, and winks at Marcia.

Lucille gets up and embraces Marcia and Charles, cooing, "It's so great to see you," and other such nonsense, when we all know she considers them below her because they're only *storekeepers*, while Uncle Dan is a lawyer. Of course, no one points out that Lucille is merely his codicil.

I excuse myself and go upstairs to phone Sean, the man I have been seeing for two months. He is spending Christmas with his parents. I need to reassure myself that I am not alone; that I am not affected by the threat of all that is familiar here in this house. By Marcia. As children, Marcia and I were two perfectly balanced halves: she, vocal, questioned everything; I, silent, trusted everything. She exposed, I concealed; she exploded, I imploded. Now, our common childhood has become disparate, each of us recalling only our particular perspectives.

I lie on the single bed I used until I left home at twenty, and dial Sean's number on the bedside phone. Mom and Dad keep my room as it was, or perhaps as they would have liked me to have kept it when I still lived here. Not a fleck of dust is visible on the glass that covers my desktop, and under which are pressed photographs and mementos of my past: a track-and-field Third Prize ribbon, my grade seven class photo, a hand-painted Valentine's heart, five PNE ticket stubs from the year I had a crush on the ferris-wheel attendant, a program of my high school prom, and a picture of William Vincent Stevenson Miller, my ex-husband, when he was eighteen.

The phone rings and rings, each hollow sound widening the gap between us, receding Sean into the past — that dangerous place in my head where doors slam shut one after another. The containment of nightmares. Like police sealing a house after a crime.

I hang up but continue to lie on the bed. Downstairs, Marcia's voice is dominant; she has, no doubt, begun. I wish I could learn to be like Uncle Dan. He is an avoidance expert. He skirts everything, and if caught in a head-on, rolls with the punch. Confrontation is like clapping: it requires two hands.

Marcia is prone to hysterical outbursts at the slightest provocation. We are all aware of this, and try not to say or do anything to upset her. Invariably though, we do. Last year, I remember, the flare-up came when Dad didn't eat all the pudding Marcia had made because he said it was too sweet. He realized immediately that Marcia was not amused, and tried to make a joke of it by saying, "Unlike you, Marcia."

This statement she interpreted as character assassination, and launched into a spiel, shouting that none of us could see her as she really was, that this family demeaned her, didn't appreciate her, and that nothing she did was right. She burst into sobs, stood up and ended her table speech by taking the bowl that contained the rest of the pudding and smashing it to the floor. Where, ironically, it didn't break, but caused a dark stain on the white rug which had Mom running to gather towels and cleaning fluids. Marcia ran out of the room, locked herself in the upstairs bathroom and continued to sob for an hour while we each, in turn, stood at the door and pleaded with her to come out, using pet names and we-all-love-yous as entreaties.

Whereas we all seem to have managed through childhood relatively unscathed, Marcia bears and displays her scars as a variety of grudges against everyone. She has a repertoire large enough to last through the next century, from which she draws at whim during these family reunions. It is difficult to imagine how Marcia has been able to document so many injustices perpetrated against her, considering she left home at sixteen.

Marcia's grudges are easily divisible into Pre-Marriage and Post-Marriage. We can be assured of at least one PreM to surface with vicious consequences, and several PostM ones, which are more recent, often the direct result of PreM animosities re-examined at these reunions.

Marcia has managed to accumulate and store enough resentment from the past to keep us all miserable and remembering. No chance of mythologizing personal history with Marcia around. Or perhaps, she has become the mythmaker in our family. We listen to her gods and demons, fueled by guilt, forgetting that some of our sins were accidental, original.

FIRST THING MARCIA SAYS WHEN I COME BACK DOWNSTAIRS is, "Good thing you didn't bring Karl or Keil, or whatever his name was."

I don't bother to reply. She is referring to a short-term lover who came with me last year. I'm not sure why I brought him to a family dinner, except perhaps out of fear that if I was alone, Marcia would single me out. Kurt was silent, uncomfortable, and happy when we left. I saw him very little after that.

Lucille crosses her legs and stares me up and down, assessing my jeans and sweatshirt, no doubt. "Come and sit here," she says in her best auntie voice. She pats a space beside her on the couch. "And tell me what you've been doing."

Slowly, they all disperse: Mom and Dad into the kitchen to start dinner; Charles, with his gin and tonic, to the family room where he watches football on TV with the sound turned off; and Uncle Dan to the dining room, rifling through files. I sit on the couch with Lucille, but I'm not listening. I'm thinking about Marcia, who is lying on the floor, flipping through an Ikea catalogue, disinterested in Lucille because she's someone with whom Marcia shares no history and thus has nothing to distort.

"Working hard?" Lucille asks.

"Yeah." Ridiculous question. How does she think I pay the rent? Lucille has never worked a day. She went straight out of high school to university where she met Uncle Dan in her second year. Passed smoothly from Daddy to Uncle Dan, like one of their briefs. Lawyer to lawyer; man to man. Twenty-six and never lived alone.

"Are you seeing someone?" she asks.

"Yes."

"What does he do?"

Marcia looks up from the floor. "What does it matter what he does?"

Lucille clears her throat and rearranges her skirt.

"He's in business," I say, vaguely. Sean writes instruction manuals for computer programs. I don't really think Lucille is interested in the details, only the salary scale.

"Is it a big business?" she asks.

Marcia sighs loudly, blowing air out of her puffed cheeks. "Don't worry," she says. "I'm sure he doesn't make as much money as Uncle Dan."

Lucille clears her throat again. She brushes lint off the arm of her sweater. "So what's so wrong about money?" she says.

Marcia rolls her eyes and begins a sermon on the evils of materialism. Uncle Dan, who is talking legal jargon into the phone, picks up the handset and carries it around the corner into the hall, which is as far as the cord will reach. Business: his method of survival. His voice, impersonal, speaks incomprehensible words and complex structures created to distance the listener. Or confuse.

I abandon Lucille to Marcia's wrath, although her eyes implore me to stay, and go to the kitchen where Mom is helping Dad make dinner. He loves to cook, is the self-proclaimed Chef in our family, and expects lavish compliments to be heaped on him as he heaps food on our plates. He also expects us to denigrate Mom's meals whenever she cooks, no matter how delicious they are. We learned to oblige early in childhood, prompted by Mom, who has perpetuated this ritual either because she is following some outdated women's credo about male ego, or most likely, to avoid cooking, which she detests. Mom hates anything domestic, including cats.

WE ARE ALL SEATED AROUND THE LARGE OVAL TABLE, WHICH Mom insisted on buying so we could all face each other. No chance of being invisible at this sitting.

"The veal is delicious," Uncle Dan says, following the rules.

"It's one of Dad's favourite recipes," I say, smiling apologetically at Mom.

Mom sighs. "I never did learn to get it as good as this," she says, beating everyone. She winks at me.

"That's a lie," Marcia says. "You're every bit as good a cook as Dad." She takes a biteful and chews slowly. "Why are you always pretending you're a failure?"

"I just had a miscarriage," Lucille says.

Dad almost chokes on his bread, and turns a shade of red.

"It's not irreconcilable," Uncle Dan jargons, patting Lucille's forearm.

"For God's sakes, Dan," Mom says. She leans across the table at Lucille. "I am sorry, Lucille. Are you all right?"

Lucille nods while toying with the potatoes on her plate.

"Well then, I'm sure you can try again in no time," Mom says, settling back into her chair. "Broccoli anyone?"

I am a little surprised, as I'm sure everyone else is too, because Uncle Dan has always made it clear that he does not want a family. Of course, no one mentions this. Dad is staring into his plate, uncomfortable with personal details of any kind.

"And Dan was so looking forward to it," Lucille says.

"Uncle Dan will make an excellent father," I say, anxious to lighten the tone. "Do you know he used to read Marcia and me stories at night, take us to parks, play all sorts of games? It was like having a second father."

"Why isn't anybody in this family honest?" Marcia says, her voice rising a notch.

I take a deep breath and let it out slowly. We have inadvertently stumbled onto another year's dispute: Marcia's inability to conceive, something she once admitted to me. Year after year, Mom has nagged Marcia on the topic of children. Finally two years ago in a hysterical exchange, Marcia informed Mom that she had been trying to get pregnant; that Charles was obviously sterile, and that everyone should mind their own business. I won't even try to explain the details or the damage.

Marcia continues to elaborate through most of dinner on Uncle Dan's shortcomings as a pseudo-father, man and human being — he is selfish and self-centred; never has wanted children; only played with us because he had to; all he ever thinks about is his work, which Dad made possible by putting him through law school; couldn't even marry a woman his own age (don't you remember what he did to Evie?); he is completely inconsiderate. As an example, she cites an incident which took place so long ago, we have all forgotten it.

Marcia has never forgiven Uncle Dan who, when she was seven, took her most favourite doll and etched in ballpoint pen, a moustache, pipe and smoke into her face. The doll was made of hard plastic and although Marcia scrubbed off the ink, she remained scarred. Marcia pronounced her dead; Uncle Dan her murderer. She laid the doll in a Barbie suitcase — white with gold embossed flowers — snapped shut the brass hinges, and turned the key in the lock. To this day, the doll lies in her coffin in the attic. Unforgotten. And Uncle Dan sits in the living room. Unforgiven. This is how Marcia is. Patient.

At the end of this, she says, "Lucille, count yourself lucky. That man would probably psychologically scar your child for life."

"Marcia! Stop it!" Mom says.

Lucille begins to cry. Uncle Dan puts his arm around her. Dad and I look at each other, then down at our plates. Mom comforts Lucille.

Charles says, "Marcia, you're being a pain."

"You're all a bunch of hypocrites!" Marcia shouts. "What about Claire's abortion?"

We are all silent, holding our breaths, the sound of her words a grenade hovering above the table, hovering above that summer long ago when Mom took me on an "extended holiday" as she referred to it, "to put this ugliness behind us." A collective agreement that it didn't happen. Marcia's eyes are wild, and I am frightened because I know this time my turn has come, and I can't escape. I look at Charles, then at Mom, begging her to do something.

Dad stands up so quickly his chair falls over. "Marcia," he says in a voice I don't recognize. "Apologize immediately." And I wonder to whom he is referring.

Marcia looks at me, at Lucille, at Charles, at Dad. He has never raised his voice to her before.

"It's all right," Lucille says, wiping her eyes with her napkin. "Marcia didn't mean anything."

But I know she did. She's right about the abortion, only I didn't think she knew. I wonder if Charles told her. I wonder how we have managed through all these years and all these reunions.

"No, Marcia didn't mean anything," Mom echoes. "Come on, everybody. It's Christmas."

Dad picks up his chair and sits back down. He gulps his wine, staring hard at Marcia, as if daring her to speak.

She pushes back her chair and stands up. "Excuse me," she says. "I'm not feeling well."

After she leaves, we make polite small talk; pretend nothing happened.

AFTER DINNER, WE TAKE OUR PLACES IN THE LIVING ROOM. Theatre sports. Improvs. Scenes choreographed through memory. Dad sits in his stuffed armchair, Mom in her antique rocker, Charles and Uncle Dan at either end of the sofa. At Mom's insistence, Lucille went up and coaxed Marcia downstairs and now they sit beside their husbands, a two-foot space as buffer zone between them. I choose the floor although there are other chairs.

Uncle Dan picks up the remote, turns on the TV and switches to CNN headline news.

"Can't you leave it alone?" Lucille says. "All you ever watch is news."

Uncle Dan elbows her lightly and she crosses her arms.

"We brought videos of our trip south," Marcia says. "We could watch those."

"There might be a movie on," Mom says. "I'll find the TV Guide." She reaches beside her on the low table, and begins to rifle through a stack of magazines. When she comes to *Better Homes & Gardens*, she is distracted from her search, and beckons to Marcia to come and see. No doubt some new renovation. The downstairs of the house is in constant mutation. Each year, surprises greet us: new furniture, new windows, new walls, new paint. Only the upstairs stays the same, preserving the past.

And then, of course, Marcia suggests we look at photo albums. I choose last year's, because I remember it as the calmest of many. Marcia gets up and comes to sit with me on the floor. When we are close like this, I am startled by how similar we are. Our hands, our bodies, interchangeable.

"What's that?" Marcia asks suddenly.

"What?" I look down to where she's pointing on my arm at the small blister where I burned myself yesterday while trying to reheat a pizza in the oven. "Accident," I say.

"Jesus, you're not still into that sado-masochistic thing you were into when we were teenagers?"

I frown. "What are you talking about?"

Lucille looks at me, startled and questioning. I shake my head at her and raise my eyebrows.

Mother says, "For Christsakes, Marcia, what are you babbling on about now?"

"Don't you remember," Marcia says, frowning, "how you used to steal cigarettes from Charles and make little burns on your forearms?"

"You've got to be kidding," I say. "Where do you get this crap?" I have an overwhelming urge to phone Sean.

"Jesus, you're a liar," Marcia says viciously. "Or a selective amnesiac." She stares at me a moment. "I bet you still have the scars. They say hair never comes back after a burn."

"Anybody want a drink?" Dad says in his terribly bright voice. He gets up and walks toward the kitchen. Marcia has never attacked him.

Marcia is tugging at the sleeve of my sweater. "Let go," I say, but not before she has exposed my upper arm and is pointing gleefully at the faint round scars.

"There," she says. "Now who's full of crap?"

"Is that what he told you?" I say quietly.

"I think I will get a drink," Uncle Dan says, and motions for Lucille to follow him.

Charles shifts in his chair. I look at him but he avoids my glance.

Mother says, "That's enough, Marcia."

"I never burned my arms," I say slowly.

"Yes you did. Yes you did. Admit it." Marcia's voice rises to a dangerous level. "Why doesn't anyone remember anything around here?"

There are only the four of us left, and unfortunately, some of us do remember what perhaps we'd rather not. Charles picks up a magazine and turns pages. I'm sure he, too, recalls those times when he would come into my room, cigarette in hand.

"Watch," he'd say, coming closer. "I can make smoke come out of my eyes. Watch carefully." His words were an incantation, setting in motion a suspension of disbelief.

The first time the lit cigarette seared my arm, I was too surprised to cry, the pain sudden and sharp as his laugh. I never told. I was in love with him, I suppose, in a childish, puppy-like way. He stopped when Marcia noticed the burns. But it was already too late.

I look at Charles now, and wonder if I should tell Marcia. To admit my own complicity, as much a betrayal of her trust as his was of mine.

"Leave her alone," Charles says.

Marcia stares at him, then at me. "This has nothing to do with you," she says. "Or does it?"

"That's enough, Marcia," Mom repeats, but her voice is uncertain.

All three of them are staring at me, Charles and Mom alarmed, Marcia waiting for me to confirm or deny a secret she is afraid exists. Like strangers approaching an accident scene, horrified and fascinated by the possibility of death. Or like us, who come together to this house each year.

"I really don't remember," I say.

Marcia's stare causes a fist of anxiety to grip my stomach. She is motionless and dangerous — a landmine I might detonate with a breath.

"Why don't I get us all a drink?" Charles says. His eyes thank me; his body uncoils. He takes large strides toward the kitchen.

"I'll get Lucille and Dan," Mom says, getting up. "Then we can all play a game of Trivial Pursuit."

Marcia sits, uncertain, disoriented by the sudden movements, the falling away of everyone. She and I the last cards of a house held together in careful balance.

"Charles?" she whispers.

I look at my arms. Marcia is right. The scars are faint, but visible. I haven't thought of them in years, more concerned with the recent, continuing afflictions of living. But then, I'm not the type of person who keeps a maimed doll in an upstairs coffin.

"Nothing happened, Marcia," I lie, softly.

Her eyes fill with tears, and I glimpse the shape of her nightmares, those frightening inescapable mirrors.

"You are so lucky," she says, covering my two hands with hers. And I'm not sure what she means.

IV. *Inside Editions*

BY MIDMORNING, I'M ON THE HIGHWAY. I HAVE TAKEN A WEEK off to go visit Marcia. I'm thankful for the rest; lately, I've been working too many twelve-hour days.

Marcia and Charles now live in Chilliwack, an hour east of Vancouver, in a house they had built. Violins and apple pie. I imagine Marcia clearing and dusting surfaces and washing floors to impress me, like children do when parents come to visit. A way of saying, *we're grownups, we're okay.* Marcia and I haven't spent much time together in the past ten years, not since she got married and I moved to Calgary and founded *Working Woman* magazine, whose logo — **WW** — connotes **Wonder Woman** and **World War**. I wouldn't be going now if Marcia hadn't called and said she was in trouble.

Just past the foothills, I roll down the window. It is June, and although the air is cool, the sun sculpts rock faces and glaciers glisten. I begin to sing: *She'll be coming around the mountain when she comes, when she comes . . .* I am an explorer driving six white horses into the wilderness; it is summer; I feel positively wonderful. Except for

Marcia, of course, I edit quickly. But the guilt only lasts a moment, because nowadays, Marcia-trouble is an oxymoron: at thirty-eight, Marcia is the perfect housewife and mother, married to Charles, the perfect husband and father. They have two adorable adopted children. They own hardware stores and homes and cars and clothes and modern everythings. Marcia is the yin to my yang: thirty-seven, divorced, university-educated and advocating independence.

She'll be riding six white horses when she comes, when she comes …

"I've been waiting forever," Marcia says, as soon as I arrive. "Hoping you'd get here before Charles gets home from work."

"What's the matter?" I ask, still in the car.

"I'm having an affair."

"You're kidding. I just booked off work, drove a thousand kilometres, and worried for two days because you're having an affair?" I begin to laugh.

"It's not funny," Marcia says and I stop laughing. "I don't know what to do."

"Oh for God's sake, talk about a cliché." I step out of the car and push the seat forward. "What does anyone do? Read a few books about it? Get a therapist? Go on a night flight to India? I don't know. You're having a midlife crisis, for God's sake. Do nothing. It'll pass." I reach into the back for my suitcase.

"You're not taking me seriously," Marcia says. "You never did take me seriously. Well, I'm not one of your *Wonder Women*!"

I sigh. I haven't felt like one myself for a while. In fact, as the years pass, either the issues are becoming more complex, or my perception is changing. *Working Woman* started out as a model for self-reliance and independence — an alternative to wife. Work as the answer. But I am starting to think that I didn't understand the question. The profiles on my desk these days convey the hardship, the stress, the breakdowns, the price of success. It's a full-time job, this commitment to production. I have to edit carefully to preserve the illusion promised by the magazine. But I am wondering if the Mrs. in front of women's names has simply been replaced by a title at the end. A trading of one jailer for another.

I put down my suitcase, and embrace Marcia, who suddenly begins to sob. "There, there," I say, holding her. "It's okay. Everything's okay. I'm sorry."

After Marcia has cried for a bit, we go inside. "I don't know how to tell him," Marcia says, and blows her nose. "But I want out."

"Are you sure?" I ask. "What about the kids?" There is something romantic and appealing about a ten-year marriage. Not exactly *WW* mag copy, but good enough for my private edition.

"Oh, let's not talk about them right now. They're with their grandparents this week. That's why I called you to come." Marcia leads me upstairs, into her bedroom. "We haven't talked for ages."

And it's true. We see each other only at family gatherings, where inner lives are edited. Marcia announces the children's latest accomplishments; Charles says they've opened a new store; I tell them the magazine's circulation has increased to 120,000. We all smile politely, not really comprehending the complexity of the statements. What it amounts to, I think, is *we're doing well*. We're *successful*. We're *progressing*.

"I've missed you," Marcia says, and collapses onto the king-sized bed.

I give up and fall backwards onto the pillows. We get under the quilt and giggle like we haven't done since Marcia got married. We recall Marcia's susceptibility to trouble. When cornered, Marcia always found a way out, and it usually involved me.

"I must have been awful," Marcia says, giggling.

"No. You were clever. The awful always happened to me." And I laugh too.

Then Marcia tells me about her lover — Tom's eleven years younger, twenty-seven, and ... well, *interesting*. To which I say, "Are we talking *intellectually* or *sexually*?" At first, Marcia protests: "He's a good talker," and "I mean, we *do* talk." Then, a sudden bubbling of giggles, contagious and uncontrollable. We are teenagers once again, before men and careers and children came between us. And much too soon, Charles is home and we sober up and put on twenty years and go downstairs.

"Look who's finally come to see us," Marcia says before Charles can ask any questions. "I couldn't believe my eyes when I opened the door."

Charles seems genuinely happy to see me. He pecks me on the cheek. "Things not exciting enough in the big city?" he says, smiling. "To what do we owe this honour?"

"I thought it was about time," I say. "The weather's great for driving, and I needed a break." Then I ask him about the business, and that shifts the emphasis to safer ground.

Later, Marcia opens a bottle of wine and orders pizza. Charles sits at the kitchen table perusing the travel section of *The Vancouver Sun*, and telling me that he's planning an exotic holiday for him and Marcia. "Without the kids," he adds.

"And just when will you find the time?" Marcia says.

"We could make the time," Charles says.

"What do you mean by exotic, anyway? I won't go where I can't drink the water," Marcia says, her voice edgy.

Charles rolls his eyes at me and continues to scan the paper. Now and then, he reads small sections out loud. Marcia is mixing a cake. The whirring and beating sounds override Charles' voice. She's doing it on purpose, I think, watching Charles for signs. But Charles continues to read, and I realize he doesn't care whether she hears him or not. They have developed foreign languages for defence.

When the food arrives, Charles turns on the six o'clock news, and we eat the pizza out of its box, without plates or utensils. It is the dinner hour also on TV. The images begin a slow longing in me. Happy families, affectionate embraces, emotional encounters — all the things I have pushed out of my life, surface on the screen and mock me. They create a barrage of needs in my head, familiar echoes I have been trying to ignore. I wish we would turn off the TV and talk. We know so little about each other, it could keep us occupied and safe for hours.

After dinner, Charles and Marcia continue to watch TV. I read a book, and make small talk in the commercials. Marcia picks up a magazine and begins flipping pages.

"Do you have to do that?" Charles asks, clearly annoyed. "I can't hear the TV above your constant shuffling."

Marcia looks up and smirks. "Why don't we go somewhere?" she says, without looking at him. She winks at me. "You know. Dancing or something. Why don't we *do* something?"

Charles continues to watch *Inside Edition*, a story about a teenager's murder attempt on her lover's wife. "Shhh," he says. "You always interrupt me so that I miss the crucial parts."

The footage shows a secret homemade video of the teenager and her twenty-eight-year-old lover. She is asking him to divorce his wife and marry her so that they will be allowed conjugal visits when she goes to jail.

"I think the car has had it," Marcia says.

Charles sighs. "Can it wait till commercial? I'm watching something."

Marcia shrugs. She continues to flip the pages in the magazine. She can't possibly be reading anything, I think, trying to make myself invisible.

"Maybe we should get a new one," Marcia says.

The teenager is now sobbing at a news conference. She is wearing a childish yellow gingham dress with a Peter Pan collar, making her appear much younger than her seventeen years. I am fascinated by the polish, the visual editing. Before the teenager actually speaks, the screen fades to commercial: a beer ad, filled with bubbles and beautiful young people laughing into each other's mouths.

Marcia looks up from her magazine and stares intently at the TV commercial. I empty the last of the wine into our glasses.

"What were you saying about the car?" Charles asks.

"Shhh," Marcia says. "I'm watching."

So, they're going to play a dumb little game, I think.

"Come on," Charles says. "You wanted to tell me something."

"Why is it I can only talk to you when you want me to?" Marcia says.

I hear the dangerous level of resentment. "Hey guys," I say.

"I'm sorry," Charles says, sarcastic. "What's the matter with the car?"

"Oh sure you're sorry. You're always sorry," Marcia says.

The *Inside Edition* logo appears and I look at the TV. While Marcia furiously turns the pages of her magazine, the teenager sobs a confession. She is so childlike and appealing that for a moment, even I, who consider myself a rational human being, hope she will not be convicted. The power of TV, I think. Too bad real life can't change camera angles.

(On the day Dad had a heart attack, Marcia was hitchhiking across Europe, and hadn't called home for three months. I gave her the news half a year later, when Marcia called from the bus station to ask for money and a place to stay. By then, Marcia's search for self had propelled her through a back-to-the-land stint, a Buddhist monk phase, and a Carlos Castaneda conversion minus the peyote. She stayed with me for six months, during which she discovered that all she'd discovered was bullshit. Having come full circle, shortly thereafter she married Charles, her high school sweetheart, and they've been living happily ever after.)

"We haven't had sex for two years," Marcia announces the next morning. She and I are in bed together, propped up against pillows. Marcia has brought us both coffee and croissants on a tray.

"But why or how?" I ask.

"I don't know. It just happened. You know. We didn't do it for a week, then a month, then before I knew it, a year had gone by and it didn't seem right any more."

I nod, but I don't really understand. It's like one of the stories in my magazine. All the guts are missing. I think about Ed — one of my longest relationships. Whatever problems we had, sex wasn't one of them. I can hardly recall what broke us up six years ago. Broke up. As if somehow we had been welded or masoned or glass-blown into one thing that suddenly shattered. I wish it had been dramatic, rather than a practical, mutual decision. Incompatibility. So scientific and final, we got busy rather than discuss it. I stopped answering the phone; left for the weekend without an explanation. We were too different, and no amount of time or discussion could have changed that. No wonder sex wasn't a problem; it was the only thing we agreed upon. I look at Marcia, trying to understand the mechanics of love. Two years. A long time to sleep alone.

"Do you think Charles is having an affair?" I ask.

"Charles? No. Not Charles. He's just not the type," Marcia says. "Besides, he's too busy with his hardware stores. I'll bet he hasn't even noticed."

"Why don't you just talk to him about it?"

"Oh Claire, you're so naive. You don't just *talk* about it. Not after all this time. Besides, I don't want to do it with him any more."

"What *do* you want, exactly?" I ask.

Marcia shakes her head. "I don't know. I want some excite-ment. I want to do more than build stuffy hardware stores." She crosses her arms.

"Charles is right. Maybe you *should* go away for a while. You can afford it. I'll even take the kids," I say, wondering if Charles' busy-ness is the cause or the effect of their problem.

Marcia picks at the raised chenille flowers in the bedspread. "Tom's thinking about going to Japan. To teach English," she says. "He's asked me to go with him."

"You're not serious?" I sit up straight. "You can't possibly be thinking of going off to Japan with some kid — ."

"He's not a kid!"

"Well, practically." I roll my eyes. "For God's sake, don't be ridiculous." I sigh. "Why did you ask me here? What do you want me to do?"

"Nothing. I don't know. I want out." Marcia pauses. "You've got to help me get rid of Charles."

You little coward, I think, but don't say so. This is what we did as kids. Two of us armed against Mom or Dad. Somehow made the owning up easier. Made the punishment more lenient — spread out over two. Halved the guilt. Well, I think, we're not kids any more. "Marcia, this is between you and Charles," I say. "You have to work this one out on your own."

(One summer, to avoid going to summer camp while our parents went to Hawaii alone, Marcia made me take off my clothes and rubbed me down with poison ivy. She convinced me that summer camp was a fearful place, and that the poison ivy itch would only last a day or so, but it would keep us home. She justified rubbing me with it, because, being older, she would be expected to recognize poison ivy. Result: Our parents cancelled their vacation; I was hospitalized for two days and feverish and swollen for a week; and Marcia was sent to camp. Secretly grateful to have escaped camp, I supported Marcia's accident story although, clearly, to react so violently to the poison ivy, I had to have been rolling in it naked. Years later, I heard Marcia tell the story at a party of how she'd gotten rid of me so she didn't have to look after me at summer camp.)

"Tom's coming over," Marcia says. She and I are lying on a blanket in the backyard, like we've done for the past two afternoons. "Just for a couple of hours."

"Marcia, please don't do that. It doesn't feel right."

"It'll be okay with you here." Marcia lies on her back and puts her hat over her face so I can't see her eyes.

"I feel really uncomfortable," I say, sitting up. "I'm Charles' guest too, you know. Couldn't you just go somewhere else?"

"I want you to meet him," Marcia says.

Tom is not my type: burly and rough and sweaty. His black tank top displays the daily workouts in the gym. We are inside where the neighbours can't see.

"So," he says. "You're Marcia's sister." His voice is surprisingly soft and his words well enunciated.

"From Calgary," I say, hesitant.

Tom slides his arm around Marcia's waist and squeezes her to him. Marcia giggles. I pick imaginary lint off my jeans.

After we've had a coffee together, when Tom excuses himself and goes to the washroom, Marcia says, "I've got some etchings to show Tom upstairs." She winks at me.

"Jesus, Marcia." My cheeks are burning.

"We'll be in your room," Marcia whispers. "*You understand, don't you? I can't do it in Charles' bed.*"

"Jesus, Marcia," I say again, furious, but Tom is back in the room.

When I hear the door shut upstairs, I pull out some magazines from the rack beside the couch. I leaf through the pages, not reading, like Marcia did a couple of days back. Jesus, I think, why am I doing cheap Marcia imitations? It reminds me of childhood, when I received what Marcia outgrew, from toys to clothes. Even, one time, a discarded girlfriend. I stuff the magazines back into the rack and turn on the TV. Then I press the volume arrow on the remote, to make sure I won't hear any moans and groans. But there's nothing to watch: soap operas and talk shows and children's puppets. *Outside editions.* I shut off the TV and stare out the window. I'd like to get in my car right now and go home. And suddenly, I see Charles' pickup coming down the street.

"Oh my God," I say, running up the stairs two at a time. I bang on the door. "It's Charles! He's coming down the street!"

There is a rustling of confusion, then Marcia opens the door, clothes hugged to her naked body. "You get in there," she says. "I'm going to the bathroom to dress."

"What do you mean?" I ask.

"You've got to pretend he's *your* lover," Marcia says, pushing me into the bedroom. "You've got to. Please." She closes the door, and I can hear her running down the hall to the bathroom.

Tom is pulling up his jeans. He keeps his eyes averted. "I'm sorry about this," he whispers. We can hear Charles calling from downstairs.

"Coming." Marcia's voice is gay in the hall.

"*You're* sorry," I say. "What are we supposed to do now?"

Tom shrugs. He is sitting, fully dressed, on the edge of the mattress. I motion him off, then make the bed. He stands, awkward, to one side. Silent.

"Well? Are we supposed to pretend we're up here talking or what?" I look at Tom, who suddenly looks too young. "Jesus, Marcia," I say once again.

"I don't know what she's told him," Tom says, hesitant. "Let's just go down and play it by ear. We don't have to tell them what we were doing."

"And just where would I have met you? I've only been here three days, for God's sake. I don't invite strange men into my bedroom." I can hear my voice begin to rise.

"All right. Listen," Tom says, his voice cool, "I don't like this any better than you do. So let's just get through it, okay?" He goes to the door and listens. From below comes muted conversation.

"You go," I say. "I'm too embarrassed."

Tom shrugs, then leaves. I tiptoe to the top of the stairs and listen. Mostly, I hear the drone of chitchat. Charles coughs and clears his throat several times. I wait until they say their goodbyes, then go to the bathroom, run a bath, get in it and lie there for half an hour. The humiliation does not wash off. What's the point of being a *WW* when I so easily allow myself to be victimized? I grab a magazine from the rack and flip through it, furious, so I don't have to think. Marcia knocks on the door six times. Finally, when my fingers and toes are completely wrinkled, I step out of the bathtub and get dressed.

On the way downstairs, Marcia stops me and whispers, "Thanks."

"Don't you *ever* do that again," I say.

Marcia rolls her eyes. Then, "Come on. Everything's okay. Act normal."

Charles, other than giving me a few strange looks, says and asks nothing about Tom. I suppose that Marcia has cautioned him. Whatever the reason, I am relieved and, by suppertime, I am starting to feel less awkward.

Later, when we are all safely settled in front of the TV, the phone rings. Marcia says, "Can you get that?" and winks.

I shrug and answer it.

"Thank God it's you," Tom says. "Get Marcia please."

"For you," I say, handing Marcia the phone.

"Hi, Janine! What's up?" Marcia says loudly. Then, she becomes serious and coos and soothes, and finally says, "All right, but only for a little while. My sister's here visiting." She hangs up and shrugs. "Janine's having a crisis," she tells Charles, and I marvel at how sincere she sounds. "I promised I'd go over and talk. I won't be long. Charles, you'll look after Claire, won't you?"

(Until she was sixteen, Marcia was only allowed to go to parties on the condition that I went with her. It was as if, even then, our parents believed I could act as talisman against trouble. Often, what happened is that I would discover there was no party — instead Marcia would take me to a coffee shop and ask me to wait there while she went out with a boyfriend. She'd return later, usually with a chocolate bar or some other bribe, and we'd sit and invent party stories to tell our parents.)

While Marcia's away, Charles and I watch two news magazines and a sitcom. Then, Charles begins to flick channels. I continue to stare at the TV for a few moments, until it becomes impossible because he's sampling channels too fast for me to grasp anything. I take out a deck of cards and play solitaire on the coffee table. An hour passes. At ten o'clock, Charles finally settles on *American Gladiators*. I look up now and then.

"Is it better?" Charles says suddenly. "I mean, with someone who works out?"

"What?"

"I mean you and Tom."

I feel my face flaming. "He's an old friend," I say defensively.

"Yeah?" Charles says and chuckles.

I bite my lip.

"It's none of my business, I know," Charles says. "Besides, there's nothing wrong with a bit of fun, huh?" He pats my back.

"No, I guess not," I say, making myself smile, when what I really want to do is shout out the truth. Damn you, Marcia, I think.

IN THE MORNING, DURING OUR BREAKFAST RITUAL, MARCIA says, "Did you get a chance to talk to Charles?"

"About what?"

"Oh, you know," Marcia says vaguely.

"No. I don't know."

"I thought you might prepare him ... you know ..."

"Marcia, I am not going to talk to Charles. If you want to talk to him, then you do it." I get out of bed. "And don't involve me in any more of your deceptions."

But later that night, after Marcia has talked Charles and me into going dancing, Tom rings the doorbell, and Marcia acts as if I prearranged it. "We're ready," she tells him. We drive to a nightclub in Tom's car. He's the designated driver, he says, because he doesn't drink much. I sit beside him; Charles and Marcia are in the back.

I haven't been to a nightclub in years. Although I hardly drink, I order and gulp a double. Anything to get me through the evening. Only two more days, I think, then I'll be on my way home. I would have left this morning, but Marcia convinced me it would seem too abrupt. At the table we are all awkward: Tom and I try to pretend we know each other (his hand on the back of my chair); Marcia chatters inanely about the people in the club; Charles listens and looks. I have just finished my second double when Marcia insists we all get up and dance. And we do, and I am thankful that I can stop pretending. I dance with Tom, stare past him at no one in particular, and think only of my body and how good it feels to move. There are a lot of things I've forgotten. I laugh and Tom laughs back. The music is too loud to talk over, and besides, I don't want to talk to him. I feel the beat inside my body, and abandon myself to the rhythm.

After several numbers, we return to the table.

"Charles is a wonderful dancer," Marcia says, trying to urge him out of the chair toward me. But Charles shakes his head.

Marcia shrugs, then quickly gets up and steers Tom to the dance floor. I sit beside Charles. He has ordered me another drink, which I sip, although I feel rather tipsy already. Charles watches Marcia and Tom; I play with the ice in my drink. A slow song begins, and Charles says, "Now this is my style." He takes my hand and pulls me out of my chair.

I don't object. Charles draws me close. I can smell his sweat. "You're a good dancer," he says in my ear. "I was watching you." His arm circles my back and presses my breasts against him.

I push him away a few inches, then look over his shoulder at Marcia and Tom, who are dancing at the other end of the room. I feel a bit dizzy. "Marcia's a good dancer too," I say.

Charles moves his hand further down to the small of my back, then presses himself against me so that I can feel the bulge of his penis. "Do you ever think about you and me making it when we were kids?" he says, his lips close to my ear.

"Charles, you're drunk." I push against his shoulders.

"I'm sorry," he says. Then, "Do you?"

"No," I say. "That was too long ago." I extricate myself from his tangle. "Let's go sit down. I feel drunk too."

Later, when we're back home, Marcia, Charles and I sit on the living room floor, drink Scotch and inspect photo albums. It's as if we're replaying an old family reunion, only in this version Marcia suddenly pulls out a diary I kept when I was thirteen.

"Where did you get that?" I say, reaching for the diary.

Marcia moves it out of my grasp and begins to read, "*Charles kissed me today. A long, lingering, passionate kiss …*"

Some children have imaginary friends; I had an imaginary love affair with Charles two years before the real one. I look at him, alarmed. He is surprised.

"Oh Marcia," I say lightly. "You remember how I made everything up in those days." I reach for the diary again.

She slaps my hand away and laughs. "Charles, I'll bet you didn't know that you were the subject of Claire's diary for months."

Charles looks at me, uncertain; I laugh, nervous, wondering how much Marcia knows or suspects.

"And she described you like one of those studs in teen mags."

Then we all laugh and once we start, we can't stop. It's partly the alcohol, I know, and partly a general giddiness — as if we're all bursting with anxiety. Laughter is an explosion of edges, an explosion of truth disguised as fantasy. Marcia and Charles begin to make up quotes out of my diary, trying to outdo each other. We refill our glasses and laugh and laugh and laugh.

"A hunk with muscles of steel," Marcia says. "Show and tell, Charles." And she undoes the buttons of his shirt.

Charles protests a little, then undoes the rest himself.

We are all drunk, I think.

"And then, his manly hand slid up her milky thigh," Charles says, and puts his hand on my inner thigh.

Marcia shrieks in laughter, and Charles quickly ventures the hand further up. He is laughing too, and I feel suddenly uncomfortable. I slap his hand away, and move out of his reach. Marcia continues to laugh, clutching her sides and rocking back and forth. Her face is flushed and her eyes excited.

I put my glass on the coffee table, and go to the bathroom. I feel dizzy and nauseated. At the sink, I splash cold water on my face. When I return to the living room, Marcia is gone and Charles is lying on the floor with his eyes closed.

"I've had it," I say. "Thank God I'm leaving soon. I could become an alcoholic around you guys. Boy, did we drink tonight." I lie down on the couch and close my eyes, overwhelmed suddenly by the weight of my head.

When I hear Charles stir, I say, "I can't move. Can you throw a blanket over me?" And I don't hear the reply, sinking into the satiny flesh of the couch.

In the night, I am wrenched from sleep by hands that move across my body. I struggle, shifting in and out of consciousness. The night is black and heavy and pressing me down, into the earth. Don't panic. Don't panic. It's only a dream. And the night is Charles, and I can't even scream because I am drowning in darkness. Don't panic. Don't panic. It's only a dream. And when I finally do manage to surface, it's dawn and I am alone.

I lie perfectly still, completely numb. At the slightest tremor, an iron band cinches my temples. I open my hand and feel the rough surface of embossed flowers. This is not my bed. Where am I? Think. Don't panic. Not here. Marcia. God, I feel awful.

The next time, I am awakened by running water and pots clanging in the kitchen sink.

"What time is it?" I ask.

"Noon," Marcia says. "I'm making coffee."

I hear the fridge door open, water pour, cups jingle — a gypsy morning, noisy and shrill. I keep my eyes shut tight.

"Did we tie one on or what?" Marcia comes into the living room. "You might want to get dressed, or cover up. Charles is on his way down."

I open my eyes and look down. I am only wearing a bra. I pull the blanket over me, quickly. "Did you undress me? I don't remember getting undressed."

"Na." Marcia yawns. "You must have got hot in your sleep."

And suddenly the dream floods through and my stomach tightens.

I wrap the blanket around me and go upstairs to my room. Don't panic, I tell myself. It was only a dream. Wasn't it? But I can feel the telltale sticky liquid in my pubic hair, lathered on my inner thighs.

Magically, I survive the coffee in the kitchen, the boy-did-I-sleep-well, the haven't-we-had-a-wonderful-time, the are-you-sure-you-won't-stay-on-a-few-more-days, and the it's-been-great-having-you part. It's not magic, really, rather active misunderstanding, like avoiding strangers by feigning incomprehension. Language connects; I dissolve meaning, reduce words to noise.

Soon, I excuse myself and go upstairs to pack. I don't want to think about last night, yet it's all I can think of. What should I have done? What did I do? I want to erase it. I want to rewind my life right back to thirteen, before Charles, before the abortion, before Marcia's suicide attempts, before I understood anything about human cruelty and deception. I want to rewind myself into a tight ball and never open. I recognize the beginning of a panic attack and make myself lie on the bed. Breathe properly. In and out. Don't panic. It'll pass.

And suddenly, Charles comes into the room without knocking.

"What do you want?" My heart is a leopard loose in my body.

Charles hesitates. "Are you all right?" He sits on the edge of the bed, and touches my leg. I jerk away.

"What's all right?" Marcia says from the doorway. She steps forward slowly, gingerly. "My, this is cozy." She crosses her arms and stares at both of us.

"I was just checking she was okay," Charles says, and stands up.

"What, with your hands?"

"I wasn't doing anything," Charles says, defiant.

"She's got a hangover and you're going to give her a physical?"

Marcia is squinting her eyes at Charles, the way our mother used to do when she caught us lying.

"Come on, Marcia, lighten up," Charles says.

"Lighten up. Sure. Easy for you to say."

"Around here it's not easy to say much of anything," Charles says. "What's your problem, anyway?"

"What's my problem? What's my problem? *You're* my problem."

"Don't start," Charles says.

They have forgotten me. I stare from one to the other, at their mouths which open and close puppetlike, controlled by the chains of resentments and deceptions. It's as if I am watching TV with the mute on. A sound erupts from somewhere inside me. Unrecognizable. Inhuman. They both turn.

"He *raped* me!" I shout. "Oh my God, how can you stand there!" I get up and run out of the room, into the bathroom, lock the door and cry and cry.

And it's all wrong because Marcia does not follow me. I can hear Charles' denial, then his retelling of the story with me as a collusive partner.

"It's not true!" I shout from the bathroom. "I was passed out."

"Get out!" Marcia shouts. "Get out, both of you. Do you hear?" She bangs on the bathroom door. "Pack your things and *get out*."

I open the door. Marcia is standing on the landing, arms crossed, face impassive. Charles stomps down the stairs.

"Marcia?" I whisper.

"That's that," Marcia says. She walks past me into her own bedroom and closes the door.

A month has passed. Everything's okay. Everything's normal. I am back in Calgary, working twelve-hour days. Today, a letter arrived from Marcia: she's selling the house and going to Japan. She writes, *You understand, don't you?*

V. *Thicker Than Water*

I ANSWER THE DOOR ONE MORNING AND FIND MY MOTHER standing on the porch — no explanation — snow collected in her hair. Before I can say anything, she pushes past me into the entrance and, after a quick look around, says, "Marcia's done it again."

"She's in Japan," I say. "What's she done now?" I don't say this in a sympathetic, sisterly tone. I say it in a I'm-sick-of-hearing-about-Marcia tone, a I'm-sick-of-having-to-treat-her-like-some-wounded-animal tone, a I'm-sick-of-everyone's-concern-directed-at-her tone. I am sick, right now, at this point in my life, of Marcia herself.

"She's back. Been back a month."

I wait.

"The wrists this time."

Even this doesn't move me. It registers in my brain as yet another Marcia machination. How many ways can she pretend to die? And how difficult could it be if she were serious? Take a look at your family, I think. We've been in a state of emergency for so long, she hasn't noticed. There's no 911 for our kind of dying. "Is she okay?" I ask, and sigh.

"Dad's with her."

"Tom?"

Mom shrugs. "You didn't really think that was going to work, did you?"

I shake my head. Eight months ago, Marcia shed us all like old skin. Exfoliated. "Why didn't you just phone?" I ask Mom.

"I promised Marcia." She sighs. "Go get dressed. I'll make the coffee."

And when we're sitting at the kitchen table, the details accumulate: Marcia wanted the children back and, when Charles said no, she dialled 911, slit her wrists, and lay in the bathtub. They found her moments later, door unlocked, water barely pink, wearing her tropical bathing suit.

"What kind of suicide is that?" I say to Mom. "She makes a mockery even of death."

"I know you're angry, Claire," Mom says in her validation tone. "And I think it's healthy for you to let the anger out."

"I'll kill her myself," I say, teeth gritted. "Shove her head in an oven, hang her from a clothesline, IV her 2000 tranquilizers. But that'd be too good for her!" And suddenly, I'm crying noisily and Mom pushes her chair up against mine and embraces and pats my back, as if I were a teenager once again, heart broken, and certain it will never heal.

"It's okay," she says. "Let it all out."

I tell her all about that night at Marcia's, before she went to Japan. I tell her about Charles. And the worst part is thinking

Marcia set it up — set me up, her sister — to get rid of Charles the easy way.

"I know," Mom says, soothing. "I know."

I sit up. "What did she tell you?"

"That Charles ... well, as you said, dear ..." She smiles, apologetic.

"I'll never forgive her," I say. "Not as long as I live."

And then she starts in on one of those guilt trips: "...Your dad ... we never know since his heart attack ...".

"You didn't tell Dad?" I shout.

"I couldn't exactly keep it from him, now could I? How else was I going to explain to him why no one is coming home for Christmas?" Her lip begins to tremble. "Oh, what have we done to deserve this?" She starts to cry and now it's my turn to comfort her.

"This isn't to do with you and Dad," I tell her. "It's between Marcia and me."

"Will you come and see her?" Mom asks.

"Never."

SO FAR, "NEVER" HAS LASTED EXACTLY FIVE YEARS. MARCIA AND I talk on the phone when it's unavoidable, pretend nothing happened. When Marcia was released from the hospital, she voided all the ugly in-betweens and set about revising our memories. She wrote me a long letter and included two articles: one on the dangerous effects of alcohol, and one on false-memory syndrome, as if I were the one trying to turn fiction into fact.

It's Mom and Dad's forty-fifth anniversary and no creative false memory can keep us from communicating, by phone at least. Neither Marcia nor I can decide what would be an appropriate gift.

The number one choice is a trip. "We thought we'd send you to Hawaii," I tell Mom.

"The greatest gift," she says, "would be for all of us to go somewhere together. As a family. Like we used to, when you were kids, remember?"

I frown. Another revisionist. I try to rewind to family trips, slow-motion running through fields of dandelions and Indian paintbrush; the four of us, picnicking at the side of a stream; weekends of gold rivers and state parks. In my childhood memories, however, Mom and Dad worked long hours and, on the weekends, family trips were low on our priority list. By the time Marcia and I were in our teens, a family outing would have been suicidal. This revisionist thing must be genetic. But instead of challenging her, I say, "Where would we go?"

"Southwestern Utah," Mom says. "You know, high desert and all those arches and cliffs? We'll rent a van."

And before we know it, it's settled and we're all headed for Salt Lake, our flights arriving within an hour of each other.

The first thing I do when I arrive is phone Lawrence at work. He's a married man I've been seeing for the past two years. Seeing. As if he were an observation, rather than an involvement.

"Is it hot there?" he asks.

"Ninety-three," I say, making it up. I haven't been outside yet. If only I'd told Lawrence about Charles and Marcia, he'd understand why I'm calling.

"I miss you, honey," he says, which sounds false, because we only see each other once a week and don't even talk daily.

"Really," I say, unable to keep the sarcasm out of my voice.

"Claire, are you okay?"

I shake my head, hang up, and practice shut off, like the switch of a furnace or a fan.

An hour later, I walk toward Mom, Dad and Marcia, fishing in my open purse for an imaginary object, to keep from looking at Marcia, who's waving to me. When I reach them, I exchange hugs and kisses with Mom and Dad, then turn to Marcia. "It's been awhile," I say.

"I love you too." She flips her head back. Marcia is thinner, more fashionable now that she's single again. Blue jeans, shoulder-length hair, makeup. She stares past my shoulder, shifts her weight foot to foot, hides hummingbird hands. My stomach clenches.

We pile into our rental van and head to Arches, Canyonlands and Mesa Verde. Dad has planned everything — he is carrying a briefcase full of maps with our exact route outlined in black felt pen; brochures in which he has highlighted points of interest, natural and unnatural history and anything he thinks we must see; a Tourbook from BCAA with alphabetical listings of locations, sights, hotels, etc., the pages of which are full of Post-it note markers; and a *Best Bed & Breakfasts of America* paperback out of which he booked our first night. He also has a notebook for his personal observations, and a lined pad to keep in the car in case of what, I can't imagine.

Marcia drives, with Mom beside her, as navigator. Of the two rows of back seats, Dad chooses the rear one so he can spread out his maps and books and read us bits and pieces of history. I sit directly behind Marcia and Mom, wondering how long it'll be before Marcia and I are alone. Almost immediately, Mom closes her eyes and dozes. I stare out the window, disoriented by Marcia's composure. She acts as if there's been no gap in our relationship, as if she truly believes in her own innocence. Dad reads out loud, whether anyone is listening or not:

> *One of the most interesting structures in Salt Lake City is the Eagle Gate. Erected in 1859 as the entrance to Brigham Young's private farm, it spans State Street. The giant four-legged arch is surmounted by a 4000-pound statue of an eagle with a wing-spread of 20 feet.*

"Dad," Marcia says, "we're not going into Salt Lake. Besides, who wants to see a statue of an eagle when we can look out the window and see real ones?"

"Where?" I ask, craning to look out mine.

"In the forest, where do you think? They're not exactly going to hang out at the freeway exits, are they? Look around, for God's sake. We're in the middle of mountains."

"The Wasach Mountains," Dad says, and bores us with facts about elevation, etc. etc. I pull *Life After God* by Douglas Coupland out of my bag and begin to read his speculations about what makes humans *human*. That they are, I think. I recall looking up the word *human* once, and being surprised to discover it simply means "pertaining to man," and that the word *humane* has a subjective meaning: "having the feelings proper to man." And what about women, I wonder. What are their proper feelings? I wonder, too, if Marcia is *humane*.

"I suppose," I say to Dad, "Wasach was some guy's name."

"It's an American Indian word meaning 'high mountain pass.'"

I'm about to ask him what makes humans human, when Marcia says, "Has anyone seen the Spanish Forks sign?" The tone of her voice makes us all straighten and pay attention, as if we have suddenly found ourselves on a tightrope.

Mom quickly reaches into the door side pocket for the map. She stares at it, without responding.

"Payston," Marcia says, reading the exit sign. "Can you find it on the map?"

Mom's still searching.

"Spring Lake?"

"Just hold on, Marcia. I'm looking," Mom says, her voice tight.

"Fuck. I've been driving for an hour and a half. It wasn't even an hour to Spanish Forks." Marcia screeches to a halt, pulls onto the shoulder and grabs the map from Mom, ripping it in the process. She points an accusing finger at it, as if the map were responsible. "There," she says. "We're fifty miles past it."

"We're supposed to be on Highway 6," Dad says, consulting his map. "Traveling smack between two national forests: Uinta and Manti-La Sal."

"Well, we're not," Marcia says. "We're traveling smack down a freeway headed for Vegas."

"Vegas?" Mom says. "Is it far?"

"Marcia, should I drive?" I ask.

"What's that supposed to mean?"

"Nothing. I just thought you might be tired."

"So, now you're all blaming me for missing the turnoff."

"Nobody's blaming you, Marcia," Mom says in her reasonable voice.

"If you take Highway 132 south, then 116 north, then 31 east ..." Dad begins.

Marcia gets out of the car and comes to the side door. We all wait. She jumps in and goes to the rear seat. "Since you know the route, Dad, you drive." She rests her head against the seat back and closes her eyes. I look at Dad who raises his eyebrows and shrugs. He gathers his maps into a pile and stuffs them back into the briefcase. Then, he steps over Marcia and goes around to the driver's seat.

After Dad pulls out, the silence in the car begins to thicken. We are being casual, coo-ool (in two syllables), terrified that the slightest sound might be interpreted as aggressive behaviour. Like walking by a vicious dog and averting the eyes.

As time passes, however, the silence settles into something comfortable around us. Two hours later, Marcia sprawls — asleep — in the back seat, Mom stares out the window, and I think that it's a good thing we took the wrong turn, because now everything is new and anything can happen.

"Children, look!" Mom says suddenly.

We all sit up, startled into obedience or out of reflex, perhaps, the word "children" plunging us back in time.

The road is newly tarred, black and shining in the hot sun. Here and there, a white feather wafts in the air. "Look, look!" Mom says, delighted.

The tiny feathers sail down to the tar and stick, fluttering like wings. More and more, until the air and the ground are black and white and fluid.

"It's a whiteout," I say.

"Tar and feathers!" Mom laughs.

"A warning," Marcia says. "Dad, are you sure it's legal to drive in Utah?"

And we all laugh and joke until we see the source of the feathers — commercial turkey farms — all those white bodies and red necks. But even this we shrug off, giddy with lack of sleep, and relief. We make Dad pull over at the first grocery store where we buy ice-cream cones and lick them all the way to I-15.

We choose the scenic route through mountain passes. There are small lakes and reservoirs in the most impossible pastels. Dad continues to drive while Marcia paints her toenails red, Mom crochets a placemat, and I stare out the window, all of us content to let Dad list facts and figures — keep things safe.

Slowly the landscape alters. We rise into the forest and lakes of a mountain pass. Then, we descend until trees become scarce, meadows yellow. The earth shows through — brown, burnt terra cotta — shrubs now spring here and there. Sagebrush. Marcia tells us she's enrolled in a Spanish night class. She spent a week in Mexico, and now wants to go live there.

"What would you do?" Dad asks.

"I don't know. Get married and have babies?" she says.

"What about you, Claire? When are you going to find a nice young man and settle down?" Dad says, missing Marcia's sarcasm.

I look out the window.

"Claire prefers other women's husbands," Marcia says.

I look up, and Mom gives me a please-just-ignore-it look. Marcia stares at her toenails and acts indifferent, as if she really were referring to my ongoing affair with Lawrence.

"I like it better this way," I say. To my right, a sandstone sculpture

— red and gnarly — rises, unexpected. Beyond it, pinnacles and buttes, abrupt and startling. Gorges and canyons. Layers of stone in undulating motion, the earth alive and moving. "It's uncomplicated and I have my independence." These words, a reflex, I've said them so often.

"I wonder if his wife would agree," Marcia says, still not looking up.

Lawrence's wife is an advertising executive who drycleans her clothes and has her hair trimmed every second week. Her bankbook is always balanced and, in her purse, she carries an electronic organizer which she actually uses. In bed, she wears a cotton nightgown with long sleeves, and she never takes off her watch, even to sleep. This, of course, is The Wife, according to Lawrence. I've never met her, but I think she must know about us, or at least wonder where he goes on Wednesday nights, when we have a standing date, regular, like work or golf. The worst part is not being able to call him when I need to. Not going on holidays together. Not having him meet my friends. Not celebrating birthdays. Not … not … not everything. His life, clean and uncomplicated, while I have only a Wednesday lover. And yet, before I left, he was anxious; wanted a full itinerary. I laughed — his jealousy, a small pleasure. Or fear, perhaps. The truth is I don't know what I'd do if he were suddenly free.

FROM THE VISITORS' CENTRE AT ARCHES NATIONAL PARK, WE begin the steep climb, switchback after switchback, over a red mountain into a startling landscape that renders us silent with wonder. Dad reads:

100 million years of erosion created this land that boasts the greatest density of natural arches in the world.

They begin to appear slowly: an animal here, a figure there — red stone surprises. Then clusters, families, castles, entire cities. It is as if we have removed an opaque layer from our retinas and we have another, more accurate vision now. A man bent over a book, a woman lying on her side, children playing in the sand, a couple kissing, the profile of a bear. Nothing is what it seems; the earth a shape-shifter. Even Dad points to rock gnomes and goblins, trusting his eyes rather than his maps and books. In some stones, we see the same creatures as if we were tuned to one satellite; in others, we perceive our own creations — monsters or angels and everything in between.

The road through the park stretches for seventeen miles, through a vast desert of red valleys and canyons, petrified sand dunes and sagebrush. Every mile or so, another point of interest: trails lead to spectacular arches and rock formations. Two hours, and Mom's already clicked three rolls of film. We choose only short trails — a mile or less — because of the heat. We are all carrying two litres of water in our fanny packs. Amazing how quickly we dehydrate in this temperature.

And this is where I see Lawrence, up ahead on the trail. It is and it is not Lawrence: a distortion, a bending of light. The sun is sweltering. I take off my sunglasses and wipe the sweat around my eyes. When I next look, he's not there. Further down, I see his features in a rock face. Once, I looked up the word *mirage: 1. an illusion visible at sea, in deserts, or above a hot pavement, of some distant object in distorted form, as a result of atmospheric conditions; 2. something illusory and unattainable.* He's following me in Calgary, I think — a superior mirage caused by the cool, dense air, mirrored to me as an inverted image. Then I think I see him behind me on the trail, but when I walk toward him, we are always the same distance apart.

We're coming back from Balanced Rock, when, in the parking lot ahead, I see Lawrence reading a newspaper in a green Hyundai. And now I know it is real, and instead of joy, inexplicably, I feel outraged, violated, as if by being here, he has broken some unspoken cardinal rule. Our relationship is defined by time and location: five hours a week, a Chinese restaurant and a Best Western on the highway. We don't belong in each other's private spaces. We don't recount our histories, don't share family albums, don't know how the other lives.

There, in the 104-degree heat, I quicken my pace. I'll go down there and tell him I don't appreciate this intrusion; this is my *family*; he's trespassing.

"Hey. Where's the fire?" Marcia asks, keeping up with me. Mom and Dad are huffing and puffing directly behind us.

"Lawrence is following me," I whisper.

"Girls, slow down," Mom says, as if we even have to walk together. "It's too hot."

Marcia turns to give her a smile. Then she leans into me. "Are you kidding? Where is he?"

"Down there." I point to the parking lot, but the green Hyundai is gone. I look up and down the road, visible for miles, but cannot see him. "Well … he was right there," I say, suddenly unsure.

Marcia frowns. "Claire, he's a jerk," she says. "Not worth imagining."

She squeezes my hand and laughs that wonderful sound that is Marcia when we were still best friends, before husbands and lovers, before manipulations, before drugs and suicide attempts, back, back so far, to a Marcia who probably only ever existed in my head.

We wait for Dad, and Mom, who is still clicking photos, as if afraid to trust her memory. But when I tell her this, she says everything here is eroding. Year to year, stone falls, ice melts into flash floods, heavy rain furrows the paths. It's all the same, yet different.

And I wonder why we are so astonished at what causes erosion: water, ice, salt — when all around us the simplest things — a word, a phrase repeated, a small gesture — are violent forces. And how we, too, are made of sandstone, of the compressed debris of our pasts, which, like salt, is unstable and shifts and buckles and liquefies under pressure.

AFTER SUPPER AT THE CASTLE VALLEY B&B, MARCIA AND I abandon Mom and Dad and descend into Moab. On the drive, Marcia quickly crams the space between us with chatter about the present: her work as a sales rep for a phone company, her new car, her wardrobe, a book she is reading, etc. I tell her about the magazine, summarize specific articles, nothing personal, not until the right moment, whatever that is. In Moab, we settle at an outdoor café and order wine.

We don't talk about Marcia losing custody of her children, of her suicide attempt, of Charles. It's enough to pretend these things never happened. Now in their teens, the children attend all the family reunions; I hear Marcia brings a succession of lovers to prove the extent of her happiness; and I, on Mom's advice and for the sake of the children, act as if there was no ugly incident.

Here and now, Marcia tells me she's made a mistake moving in with her new lover. "I was afraid of being alone," she says, candid, and shrugs. He has already been unfaithful to her, although whether this is only Marcia's version, I can't tell. I give her stupid, obvious advice: move out.

Two young men get out of a car and walk down the middle of the street, one following the other, looking clean and *good*, like most of the teens we see here in Utah.

"When are *you* going to get a real life, Claire?" Marcia says, quickly swerving the topic. "Trust a guy for a change."

"I haven't found the right one," I say lamely.

"I don't know, Claire. You don't seem to have any problem finding the wrong ones."

And what can I say to that? She's right, and it's infuriating because she always manages to zero in on that soft underbelly. The kind of thing we're all too polite to do.

I am saved from a reply by the boys on the street who stop, suddenly, face to face. One shoves the other on the shoulder, shouts. The other steps back, arms waving in the air. Soon the boys are performing an agile dance in front of us — like Tai Chi, no contact, lots of give, only there's shouting to accompany the moves. And it makes me think Marcia and I are doing just this, only we don't shout out loud. And I wonder what would happen if we really did start shoving, and who would go over the edge?

It's past eleven when we begin the drive back to the Castle

Valley Bed & Breakfast — a forty-minute drive along a winding road skirting the Colorado River, then up a thousand feet into a verdant valley. When we shut the car doors, an impenetrable barrier drops between us, making it impossible to speak. I drive, and practise opening lines: *Why have you always victimized me?* No. Too clinical. *You're a selfish bitch.* Too cold. *How could you do such things to your own sister?* Too wimpy. *Don't you care about me?*

In daylight, the canyon here forms castles and mesas of red burnished stone, with the Colorado River on our left as moat. Easy to imagine medieval knights and maidens. Right now, however, it's dark and the walls are ominous, foreboding — like driving through a crack in the earth.

Up ahead to our right, suddenly, a burst of artificial light. Then, just as quickly, the light pans across the road, across the river, and illuminates the other side. At first, I think it must be search-and-rescue. A helicopter, perhaps, though I don't see or hear one. Then I recall the brochure, the night raft trip, complete with guide to interpret the terrain. On the road up ahead, we see a truck with a bank of Hollywood lights mounted on its front. A lightman aims the lights at the formations being discussed. I pull over and park facing the river.

Marcia sits quiet, too quiet. The silence expands to a torturous level.

"Marcia," I begin, finally.

"Don't talk, Claire," she says, pressing her fingers into her temples.

"I'm going to talk, and you're going to listen," I say.

"No, I'm not," she says in a childish voice. "You can't make me." She covers her ears.

I grab her fingers and yank them away from her head. "Did you set me up?" I am coiled tight, brimming with years of frustration.

Marcia presses herself against the window.

"I need you to tell me you didn't set me up." I shake her. "Tell me you didn't."

But Marcia opens her car door and flees. "I can't stand it any more," she says.

I follow her down the few feet to the river, in the sultry night air, repeating, "Tell me!" The raft meanders slowly downstream. In the moonlight, we can see eight people who begin to wave, as if we were friends.

"Why does everyone blame me for everything?" Marcia says.

It happens so quickly. She slides out of her sandals and runs into the water. Then, she's swimming toward the raft.

"Come back here," I shout. "I'm not finished with you!" I am shaking and crying. "You can't just fuck off when things don't go your way!"

But Marcia's splashing away in a dramatic escape and, for a moment, I think, I'll get back in the car and drive off. Let her drown and float down the Colorado to the Pacific. I'll pick up Mom and Dad and we'll have a great holiday.

Then, just as quickly, I sense danger. Marcia is halfway out. Neither of us is a good swimmer; there may be currents and whirlpools. "Marcia, hang on!" I cry out, my voice trembling. "I'm coming." I dive in, and my fear of water dissolves, and all I can think of is *Please, let Marcia be all right. She's my sister, no matter what.* The raft lays anchor and two men dive into the water, carrying life preservers. I thrash around, my clothes weighing me down, when I hear the lightman dive in after me. He reaches me easily and pulls me back to shore. I call Marcia's name, my voice echoing against the canyon walls. The truck now shines its banks of lights at the river, and it feels as if we're filming a movie out of sequence, and I don't know where or how this part fits in the story.

Take one. Take two. I watch the men help Marcia across the water, into the raft, and she is saved and everyone on the raft cheers. I can almost imagine the words, *The End,* only in this movie Marcia shouts, "Get the fuck away from me!"

I smile apologetically at the lightman, who is still gripping the handlebars of his bank of lights, aiming them at the raft that is now coming toward me, as if he were making a documentary of a search-and-rescue.

"Did she fall?" he asks.

"Not exactly," I say. "Sort of." And I think about falling, only with Marcia it's more a deliberate dive, as if the treasure were only at the bottom.

The raft stops in front of us. Marcia steps out and wades through the water, stage lights on, and emerges like a goddess of the sea. And I can feel the magic, the madness all around. Marcia comes to me, embraces me. She puts her head on my shoulder and begins to sob. "I'm sorry," she repeats, over and over, while I stand there, wanting to comfort her/me, but desperately afraid, embarrassed by this proximity, this exposure. And I think about mirages and how they really can be seen at night, because all you need is the bending of light, and you can do that in your head, with memories. And I think, wouldn't it be great if our past were just a distortion caused by atmospheric conditions?

OUR LAST STOP IS MESA VERDE NATIONAL PARK — THE CLIFF dwellings of the Anasazi. Mesa Verde: green table. From below, it looks uninhabitable — a stone cliff. As we wind up, up and around switchbacks, it changes, or my perception of it changes. The massive rock walls are really a tapestry of canyons whose insides we can see. Nothing is solid, like I imagine all matter is supposed to be. The darker shades of rock are really shrubs and burned-out junipers. There's been a forest fire here recently — the park reopened yesterday, they tell us at the gate. When we reach the top, we're at 8500 feet, and none of us has elevation sickness. Below us, we can see hundreds of miles of lush farmland, shades of green. Around us, everything's black — charred tree trunks and ebony ash.

We buy tickets to Balcony House and wait in line, under a fiery sun. Both Marcia and I have forgotten our hats in the car. We search for shade nearby and find a small area, in front of which is a tidy pile of branches. Marcia and I step on these to get to the cool behind.

"You're not supposed to be there," the ranger says, sternly. "That's why the barricade."

Marcia and I look at each other, make faces, and come down. Dad rolls his eyes; Mom smiles; we stifle laughs. Interesting that what we saw as a step was really a barricade.

To get to Balcony House, the ranger explains, we'll have to descend two hundred feet, then climb a thirty-two-foot ladder. To get out, we'll have to squeeze through a small tunnel on our hands and knees, then climb back up to the top.

"I don't know," Mom says. "I think I'm claustrophobic."

"No, you're not," Dad says. "Remember the grottos in Italy?"

"That was me, Dad," I say. "Mom stayed at the hotel with Marcia."

"I remember the grottos," Marcia says. "I was the claustrophobic one."

"I don't think so, Marcia. Weren't you a baby?" Dad says.

"No. It was Claire who was the baby ..." And on and on and on as we descend the steps, then the trail. Climb up the ladder and there it is, Balcony House: like a medieval castle built in and around a natural cave in the side of a cliff — stone walls and windows, turrets and towers.

The guide tells us the Anasazi moved from their dwellings on top of the mesa, into the cliffs. They lived here from seventy to a hundred years, then disappeared. Some say they traveled on, and were absorbed into other cultures; others say a twenty-four-year drought forced them out of the cliffs; still others say a catastrophe happened and they all died. Versions, everywhere.

"It looks so difficult," Mom says, "to get up and down. Why would they choose to live here, when they could have lived below in those fertile valleys?"

"Human nature," Dad says. "Fear."

Marcia and I stare over the edge of the eight-hundred-foot drop.

"Some balcony, huh?" Marcia says.

Acknowledgements

These stories have appeared in the following magazines and anthologies:

"Beauty Foils Rapist" and "Fugue" in *Room of One's Own;*

"How To Behave," "Versions" and "The Savage God" in *The New Quarterly;*

"Los Desesperados" in *STORY;*

"Tabloids" in *Rampike;*

"Measures" and "Rondeau" in *NeWest Review;*

"Versions" in *The Journey Prize Anthology*, *Brass Tacks*, *The New Quarterly*, translated into Chinese in *Hong Kong Literature Monthly* and *Translit;*

"Snake" and "Fear" in *Event.*

"The French Woman" and "Family Reunions" were finalists in the CBC Literary Competition.

Some of the music forms and word definitions come from *The Concise Dictionary of Music* (Wm Collins Sons & Co, 1984), *The Canadian Oxford Dictionary* (Oxford University Press, 1998), and *The Concise English Dictionary* (Omega Books, 1985).

Many thanks to my editor Barbara Kuhne for her sensitive reading and editing, my agent Carolyn Swayze for her continued support and Frank Hook for everything and more.

PHOTO CREDIT: SUZANNE GUEST

About the Author

Born in Trieste, Italy, Genni Gunn is a writer, musician and translator. She is the author of four works of fiction, including a recent much-praised novel, *Tracing Iris*. Her novel, *Thrice Upon a Time*, was a runner-up in the Canada/Caribbean category of the Commonwealth Prize for the Best First Novel in 1990. Gunn was also a finalist for the CBC/Saturday Night Competition from 1995-1998 in the fiction and personal essay categories. Her collection of poetry, *Mating in Captivity*, was shortlisted for the Gerald Lampert Award, and her translation of Dacia Maraini's poetry collection, *Devour Me Too*, for the John Glassco Translation Award. She has written a libretto for Vancouver Opera and her prose and poetry have been widely published and anthologized.

Genni Gunn has a BFA and MFA in Creative Writing from the University of British Columbia and has taught many creative writing workshops. She lives in Vancouver.

Mount Appetite • by Bill Gaston

Astounding stories by a writer whose work is "gentle, humorous, absurd, beautiful, spiritual, dark and sexy. Gaston deserves to dwell in the company of Findley, Atwood and Munro as one of this country's outstanding literary treasures." — *The Globe and Mail*

1-55192-451-X • $19.95 CAN • $15.95 USA

A Reckless Moon and Other Stories • by Dianne Warren

A beautifully written book about human fragility, endorsed by Bonnie Burnard. "Warren is clearly one of a new generation of short-story writers who have learned their craft in the wake of such luminaries as Raymond Carver and Ann Beattie ... Her prose is lucid and precise." — *Books in Canada*

1-55192-455-2 • $19.95 CAN • $15.95 USA

A Sack of Teeth • by Grant Buday

This darkly humorous novel paints an unforgettable portrait of one extraordinary day in the life of a father, a mother and a six-year-old child in September 1965. "Buday's genius is that of the storyteller." — *Vancouver Sun*

1-55192-457-9 • $21.95 CAN • $15.95 USA

Small Accidents • by Andrew Gray

Twelve dazzling stories by a Journey Prize finalist. "Andrew Gray tells tall tales that tap into the hubris of the human condition ... He expertly depicts the gore of human error and conveys a present as startling as a car wreck." — Hal Niedzviecki

1-55192-508-7 • $19.95 CAN • $14.95 USA

What's Left Us • by Aislinn Hunter

Shortlisted for the Danuta Gleed Award. Six stories and an unforgettable novella by a prodigiously talented writer. "Aislinn Hunter is a gifted writer with a fresh energetic voice and a sharp eye for the detail that draws you irresistibly into the intimacies of her story." — Jack Hodgins

1-55192-412-9 • $19.95 CAN • $15.95 USA